MASTER OF REVENGE

SIENNA SNOW

GODS OF VEGAS - BOOK 3

BY SIENNA SNOW

Copyright Page

Cover Design: Steamy Designs

Editor: Jennifer Haymore

www.siennasnow.com

ISBN - eBook - 978-1-948756-12-9

ISBN - Print - 978-1-948756-23-5

DEDICATION

Many people wish for a tribe, a group of friends who support you through thick or thin, celebrate even the smallest of achievements, push you to strive for the stars, and make you laugh through the darkest of times. I can say, I am blessed to have three amazing authors (The Novel Sirens) in my life, who mean the world to me. Aliza Mann, Sage Spelling, and MK Schiller without you ladies I'd never have come as far as I have. Thank you for being my rock and allowing me to be yours.

If you would like to know more about the fabulous women who comprise the Novel Sirens, find us in our reader group: https://www.facebook.com/groups/TheNovelSirens/

CHAPTER ONE

Henna

"OH GOD, what did I do last night?" I moaned to myself as the sun streamed over my face, making me squint.

I never forgot to close the blackout curtains. I couldn't have drunk that much.

I shifted on the bed and whimpered. Everything hurt. My back, my arms, my... That was when it hit me.

I turned to the side and found the most breathtaking and exasperating man I had ever known sleeping next to me.

Oh God, I didn't.

The discomfort and arousal I felt between my legs told me I definitely had. Multiple times, as I recalled.

Shit, shit, shit. What the hell was I thinking, taking Zacharias Lykaios to bed?

He was the enemy.

Hot as hell with a body made for sin, but an enemy nonetheless.

It was supposed to have ended at the poker table as it always had before. Win, take his money, flirt, and leave.

As with most of our high-stakes poker games, we were the last two left at the table, the other players having bowed out hours earlier. I was just about to call when Zack had added a night I'd never forget to the pot. It was a dare. He knew he was about to lose and he wanted me to collect. So I raised him, with a night to let him do whatever he wanted with me. That was when a gleam entered his eyes and he set his cards on the table.

Royal flush.

I'd been had. It was his first win against me in over six months.

When he'd offered me his hand, I'd slid my palm over his and followed him out of the poker room.

I studied his face, resisting the urge to stroke his stubble-covered jaw. Dark hair cut in a way that made him look young yet professional, face that looked like he was sculpted by the Greek gods, and a body built like a fighter, all honed, lean muscles. Then there were the tats he hid under those tailored suits.

I had to stop ogling him and get the hell out of here.

Fuck, and where was here?

I lifted my head.

The room was all shades of gray with splashes of blue and black, very masculine.

Zack's penthouse. At the Aegis.

This was just great.

There was no way I could leave this hotel without anyone noticing me. I was too recognizable.

I shimmied my way off the bed. That was when I noticed the silk ties attached to the headboard.

My cheeks heated. Zack had made good on giving me a night I wouldn't forget, as I had in letting him do whatever he wanted to me.

My body hummed, wanting to relive the night.

This was so bad.

I pushed back the thought and began to search the floor for my clothes. That was when I found my dress torn in half. The memory of Zack's frantic hands filled my mind, of him trying to work the buttons on the back of my dress and then giving up and ripping the beaded sheath off me.

We'd been so frenzied to get naked. We hadn't even made it to the bed. It had been hot, sweaty, and all-consuming.

I quickly bit my lip as a groan almost escaped my lips. *Snap out of it, Henna.*

I rushed into Zack's closet, yanking a T-shirt from a

hanger and slipping it over my head before I rummaged through the drawers until I found a pair of jogging pants. I folded and rolled the waist to keep them from falling. It was the best I could do. The man was twice my size.

I tiptoed from the bedroom, catching sight of my purse and heels sprawled in the hallway leading to the entryway of the penthouse. I slipped on my shoes, grabbed my clutch, and made my way to Zack's private elevator.

I sighed, glancing over my shoulder one last time, in the direction of the room Zack slept in. If only circumstances were different.

I stepped inside the lift, knowing I'd have to deal with the aftermath of one reckless night sooner or later.

IT TOOK me a good forty-five minutes to make it back to my house. I'd looked ridiculous in my thousand-dollar heels and Zack's workout clothes, but no one seemed to pay attention, or if they had, they hadn't let on. Hopefully no one associated me with the always impeccably dressed and professional Henna Anthony.

Thankfully, my driver/bodyguard/keeper, Brandon, was waiting for me the second I stepped out of the back entrance of the casino side of the Aegis Hotel and Casino. He hadn't batted an eye at my crazy getup and drove me home.

"Will you need me later today for our normal routine or will you take the day off? It's a shame you never take time to enjoy the beautiful house you had built."

I wish I could take a day off. In my world, sleep, rest, and fun were commodities I couldn't expect. Stolen hours hanging out with my best friends were the most I could expect. I was in the business of providing enjoyment for others, from college kids trying to blow off steam to oil billionaires from the Middle East.

"You know there's no rest for the weary. We have some high rollers coming in tonight, and they expect a personal welcome."

Brandon shook his head. He was handsome, with salt-and-pepper hair and a six-foot-five height. He had a very distinguished older vibe that caught the eye. "I'll be here at four. At least get some sleep."

"That's the plan. Once I review a few contracts and make some calls, the bed is where I'll go."

"You are stubborn, Miss Anthony."

I smiled, stepping out of the SUV. "Did you just figure this out? You're getting rusty, Brandon."

He shook his head again. "See you soon."

My garage opened as I approached, revealing Blane, one of the security details. Collin, my boss at Lykaios International and surrogate father, had insisted I remain vigilant in my personal protection from the time I was a child, and now that I ran his empire, it had become second nature to have people around me.

"The property is secure, Ms. Anthony. Enjoy your rest." Blane nodded to me.

"Thank you."

The second I crossed the threshold of my house, I released a sigh. Finally, I could be myself.

The house smelled wonderful. Gardenias. My favorite flower.

I stared across the open entry into the vast sunroom which opened to a garden oasis in the backyard. This palatial home was my splurge, my gift to myself for all the sacrifices, all the pain, and all the damage of the past.

My house was part of a twenty-thousand-acre development I owned on the outskirts of Vegas. It sat on a fifteen-acre plot that served as my respite from the hustle and bustle of the Strip.

I'd found the land during my freshman year at the University of Nevada, Las Vegas. Penny had come home from college with a few of her friends and we'd decided to go hiking in the caverns about an hour outside of Vegas. On our way home we stopped at a hole-in-the-wall diner where the owner, an older lady, talked about all the land her recently deceased husband had left her and how she wanted to sell it off.

From as far back as I could remember, I knew real estate was the way to make my mark in the world. I also knew that I couldn't afford anything in the various popular areas of Vegas. My only hope was to buy a diamond in the rough.

So I convinced everyone to make a detour to see the property. There was nothing but desert, no land infrastructure, no anything. There was barely a one-lane dirt road. The only sign of life was the distinct silhouette of Las Vegas in the distance.

I wanted it, and no amount of convincing from anyone was going to keep me from getting it. I saw a potential no one else could.

I'd stayed in touch with the owner and told her I was interested in purchasing her land. I knew she'd thought I was crazy for wanting it, and even more so when I came back to her two years later with a cash offer for her insanely large property.

It had taken me another three years to have the land developed, and now it was one of the most coveted communities in the Las Vegas area, with the average home prices being in the tens of millions.

Most people had no clue I was the mastermind behind the community, and I was fine with it. Especially since I couldn't tell anyone that the money for my project came from my winning in underground and highly illegal poker tournaments where hundreds of millions changed hands with a draw of the cards.

My phone rang as I kicked off my shoes and walked toward my kitchen.

Checking the display, I saw the call was from my baby sister, Anaya.

She was on an internship in Geneva. Every time I talked to her, there was a sense she was homesick. We were close as any sisters could be. We'd survived the crimes of our deceased father, a notorious embezzler with a list of enemies a mile long who'd committed suicide instead of facing justice for his crimes. This was the first time in her life we'd been apart for more than a month. I missed her like crazy, but her internship was an opportunity less than one percent of all applicants received.

"Hey there, little sis. How's Europe?"

"Kicking my ass. I'm so tired."

"You and me both."

"Long night for you. Who did you have to wine and dine? A sultan, or was it a reclusive billionaire, or maybe it was a hot-as-sin businessman?"

God, if she only knew.

"We had a few whales in house. Tonight's the one I'm dreading. We have a group of European aristocrats coming to celebrate a bachelor party. I'll be lucky if I get any sleep for the next two days. Then there's the show in less than two weeks I'm preparing for."

"Oh yeah, the Las Vegas International Auto Show. I love walking through all the exhibits. I'm going to be so jealous if you get to drive the new Lamborghini the magazines are talking about."

One of the perks of the show moving to Lykaios Arena was having the privilege of driving some of the cars.

"I promise to keep my joyriding all to myself."

"Whatever. That means you're already scheduled for a drive, or at least a ride-along."

"My lips are sealed. Collin's the one I need to keep from getting behind the wheel. He's as much an adrenaline junkie as I am."

"You're making sure Collin isn't doing too much, right?"

Collin Lykaios was the one person outside of our mom who Anaya and I loved with all our hearts. He'd protected us, literally, from the world and had sacrificed his life, his family, for us. I could never repay the man for all he'd done or the secrets he'd kept. He was my father in all things but blood.

"Yes, Anaya, I'm making Collin jump out of airplanes and work his fingers to the bone. It's only fair he puts in the same hours I do since he owns the place."

"You're such an ass," she huffed. "I miss him. I miss you and Mom."

Her tone had me worried.

"Ana, did something happen?"

"Nothing bad. It's just this job is harder than I expected. I feel like I've joined a cult."

My baby sister was a bookworm to the max, and I had a feeling interacting and being social was her main issue.

"Marketing and social media analysis isn't all behind the scenes, I take it?"

She snorted. "Not even close."

"It'll be okay. One more month and you'll be back home. Just in time for Penny's wedding."

Persephone Kipos was our cousin and all-around amazing woman. She was set to marry Hagen Lykaios in a little under six weeks. It was going to be a fusion of Penny's Indian and Greek heritage. Penny wanted her wedding to be a celebration of the traditions of her Indian mother, my aunt, and her Greek father.

"I can't wait. It's going to be so much fun. Plus, now I'm old enough to drink and can party it up with you."

"Yes, yes. I bet you've been restraining yourself for the last few months."

"I haven't had a sip of alcohol. It's part of my contract. It was a bit of a bummer not to have champagne on my twenty-first birthday. But as you say, work is work, and we have to do what we have to do."

My words sounded depressing. I needed to figure out something a little more inspiring.

"So, I heard a rumor."

"I'm listening."

"Well, not really a rumor since it was confirmed. Penny said you left a fun party to play poker with Zack."

I yawned, deciding bed was a better option than work.

"Penny is a gossip."

"So, it's true?"

"It was business. We had to organize a high-stakes game between his whales and mine. It's a long story but the players are all friendly rivals. Both the Lykaios Casinos and the Aegis Casinos made out big so that's all that matters."

It was also the reason Zack and I ended up at a late-night poker game, and what led to us screwing each other's brains out.

"Did you hit it?"

"What?"

"I'm just saying. Did you finally jump Zack? It's like watching two feral animals circling each other."

"I take offense to that."

"You didn't deny it."

"Ana, I do not have time for a relationship."

"I'm not talking marriage and babies, although you are getting there in age." The humor in her voice made me want to shake her. I was only twenty-seven. "I'm talking about getting serviced by him. The brothers are known for their mad skills in the sheets."

"You need to stop reading tabloids and focus on school and work."

"Yet again, you didn't deny it."

"I'm going to bed. You're giving me a headache."

"I love you, sis."

"I love you too, squirt."

"I'm taller than you by five inches. I'm not the squirt."

"Yes. You're so smart. Now I'm off to bed." I paused. "Ana, if you want to come home, I'll send Collin's plane this minute."

She sighed. "No, this is something I have to do. From what I hear, surviving the internship is the hardest part of working for the firm. After it, I'll have a job waiting for me as soon as I graduate. I'll pay my dues and then get paid bank when I officially start working for them."

"Good. We all have to pay dues to succeed."

"Do you think you'll ever stop trying to repay Collin for all he did for us and live your life? He doesn't expect anything in return, Henna. He wants you to be happy."

I froze. "That subject is not open for discussion, Ana."

"You never want to discuss it. You aren't the only one who owes him something."

"Anaya." I gave her my I'm-your-big-sister voice.

"Fine. Get some sleep. I'll call you in a few days."

CHAPTER TWO

Zack

I STRETCHED, rolling to my side as the haze of alcohol and sleep lifted from my mind.

"Henna," I murmured, wanting to lose myself in her one more time before I started my day.

Never in a million years had I expected a game of cards would lead to the most incredible and erotic night of my life. We'd played against each other countless times over the past several years without it leading to anything more than eye fucking and trying to win the pot at poker.

Last night, I couldn't pinpoint what had come over me, but I'd dared her and she'd stepped up to the challenge, giving me the reality of all my cravings and fantasies.

She was a fucking goddess, demanding her pleasure

and giving up control all at the same time. And God could the woman kiss.

My cock strained hard, wanting to bury deep inside Henna's silky, wet heat.

"Henna. Come here." I lifted onto my elbows, expecting to see her sleeping on the other side of my bed.

There was no one.

I checked my clock—it was noon. Sleeping in wasn't unusual when a night as one of the casino owners lasted into the early-morning hours. The fact Henna and I hadn't fallen asleep until seven should have meant she was too tired to move. Hell, I'd fucked her four times.

I wiped my hand across my face and threw back the covers. Strolling from the bed, I searched my penthouse. Maybe she was drinking coffee.

Nearly everyone she interacted with knew her addiction to coffee. I stepped into the kitchen with no sign of her.

Hell, there was no trace of her anywhere, except the lingering scent of the jasmine-tinged perfume she favored.

This couldn't be fucking happening. She left me without a backward glance. No note, nothing.

I clenched my jaw.

If she thought it was going to end with one night, she was sorely mistaken.

"MR. LYKAIOS, everyone is waiting for you in the conference room," my personal assistant Simon said as I entered my office.

I braced myself for the scowls I was sure to get from my brothers, Hagen and Pierce. I was an hour late for a project meeting between HPZ, the conglomerate owned by me and my brothers, and Lykaios International, the corporation owned by my estranged father, Collin Lykaios, and run by Henna Anthony.

Thinking of her, I pushed down a wave of irritation from the disappearing act she pulled the other night and adjusted my suit jacket as I followed Simon into the conference room.

This was the last place I wanted to be but I had to suck it up. The profit from the joint venture project of three South Pacific destination resorts would be double what we'd made from any property investment to date.

It burned to know my brothers had rekindled a relationship with the very man who'd thrown us out on our asses when we were barely eighteen and now were fine doing business with him. Then again, both men were in different phases of life.

Hagen was about to marry his dream girl, and Pierce was a father and engaged to the love of his life, Amelia Thanos. I was positive their wedding was going to be as big as Hagen and Penny's, if not bigger. Well maybe not— knowing Pierce, he'd probably convince Amelia to elope.

Then, there was the fact the woman who'd blown my mind two nights ago and left me without a backward glance was sitting in the same room as my family made me want to punch my fist into a wall.

Damn her, I could still taste her on my lips. Hell, I could still feel her cunt clenching around my cock as she came.

Never in my life had a woman left me. I was the one slipping out before my lover woke.

The second I stepped into the room it fell abruptly silent.

"Sorry for the delay. I had a meeting that ran over."

I kept my gaze on my brothers, not acknowledging Collin or Henna.

Fuck, the only seat available was across from them.

"You're just in time to go over the final provisions before we execute." Hagen passed me a folder. "The highlighted areas are where we need your signature. Pierce and I just signed our copies, as did Collin and Henna."

I scanned the contracts. Everything looked standard for any high-priced development. My lawyers had done their preliminary study last week and I knew everything was on the up-and-up. That was when I came to a spot where it said a team comprising members from HPZ and Lykaios International would oversee the first development on the island of Bora Bora that was set to start in less than two months.

"Who will make up the team going to Bora Bora?" I glanced at my brothers, but Henna answered.

"We're working out the logistics." The sound of Henna's honey-smooth voice made my cock jump and pissed me off further. "Hagen has given me a list of names from HPZ and I have a list of associates qualified for the project. I'll spend two weeks with the team getting them oriented and then return to my normal duties here at Lykaios."

I lifted my gaze from the documents and locked my eyes with Henna's chocolate depths.

There was a flicker there as her mouth opened to release a slow breath. Oh, she was picturing everything we'd done the night before last.

And it was going to happen again and again.

"Who will handle your responsibilities while you're gone?" I asked, not really caring.

Lykaios International was the legacy my brothers and I were supposed to inherit. What was the point of Collin spending every waking moment of my childhood working to give us financial stability when it ultimately destroyed our family? I planned to dismantle it piece by piece rather than let it go to anyone else.

"My VP will hold down the fort. She's up to date on how to handle all the Lykaios International properties."

"I'll join you. I want to make sure this project goes off without a hitch."

"Zacharias, this is Henna's development, and as per the contracts, she runs the show."

I hated when Collin said my full name. I'd avoided any contact with him for years and now I had to work with him.

I focused on my father. Blue eyes that looked almost sapphire, dark hair with a peppering of white, and a body that looked anything but frail for a man in his sixties. That was when it hit me. He was exactly what I'd look like in thirty years or so. There was no denying my genetics. Hagen was a combination of both my parents and Pierce resembled our mother, but me—I had to get the bastard's looks.

"It also says any of us have the right to visit the project site whenever we see fit."

I knew I was being an asshole. Hagen was probably going to kick my ass. The man was a former mob enforcer and built like a tank, so I wouldn't be able to take him, but I'd give him a good fight.

"Son, what about this project concerns you? This is standard procedure for any development." There seemed to be genuine concern on Collin's face.

Why the fuck would he care?

I clenched my jaw. "I'm not your son. You made that clear ten years ago."

Collin visibly winced and immediately Henna set a

hand on his arm, whispered something to him, and then turned her attention on me.

The impact of her anger hit me. She was so calm all the time that when she lost it, she had a reputation for eating her victims for lunch.

"Listen very clearly, Mr. Lykaios. This project was brought to your attention because Collin thought it would be a unique venture to bring all of his sons into the mix. Don't ever mistake his generosity as a weakness and think it leaves him open for you to take jabs at him. If you find the terms we offered unreasonable, then you are free to pass on the deal. We do not now nor have ever needed your capital."

"Stop being a jackass, Zack." Pierce glared at me. "You either sign it or get out. This isn't about you or your issues with Collin. It's about making sure my son and any other children the three of us have are set for the future."

Well, fuck, bringing Christopher into it changed everything. I loved my ten-year-old nephew. The boy had a way of even making my grumpy ass smile. I had to calm down.

"I'll sign but I plan to be there when they break ground."

"That doesn't make sense. Only one of us needs to be there to oversee the start of construction. Besides, Charlie is the construction manager and has experience with projects on a bigger scope than ours. Too many executives will make it seem as if we don't have confidence in her abilities."

Who was Charlie? And who gave their daughter a man's name?

"Have I met Charlie? Who vetted her?"

Henna glared at me. "Charlie is Charlotte Steel. Charlie is her preferred name. I believe you used her on your Paris project."

Damn. How could I have forgotten? Charlotte... Charlie would kick my ass if I interfered when she worked. The woman was the size of a pixie but with balls bigger than a land barge. She was one of the best in her field and getting her to head up the project meant she was vested in its success. And in Henna.

Charlie was known for passing on a project if the higher-ups weren't up to her standards. No amount of money could make her change her mind. It was rumored she was a heiress to a Norwegian oil fortune but had turned her back on it when she found out her family was in business with a company linked to Russian drug traffickers.

"Charlotte is the best. I have no issues with her."

"Then what is the problem?" The tone of Henna's voice told me she would meet any challenge I posed head-on.

My erection grew harder. Hell, my cock was never going to go down.

Why it always turned me on when she drew her claws

was beyond me. The undercurrent of attraction had sizzled between us for over five years. We'd never acted on the attraction until last night. No, that wasn't true—I'd given her a kiss a few months ago when I couldn't figure out how to get her to leave one of Hagen's clubs after a night out with Penny and Amelia. She'd been drunk and her temper was at an all-time high because the boys had crashed girls' night. She'd crawled under my skin that night and all I'd thought of doing since was getting between her legs.

"There isn't a problem, per se. I believe my presence in Bora Bora will give a unified front for this joint venture. It'll be a great opportunity for publicity, especially since the public views our companies as rivals."

Henna lifted a brow, as if saying, "We are rivals." Instead of responding, she leaned over and spoke to Collin. Whatever he said to her had her frowning and then releasing a deep sigh before nodding.

"So you're proposing a marketing op?"

"Yes. It is widely known we own a successful resort on the northern end of Bora Bora and any expansion of our presence in the area won't go unnoticed. Plus, since I'm in talks to purchase Remy Bora Bora and you're using the property on extended lease as the base for all those involved in construction instead of our property, it'll show a united front. Especially if the sale goes through before construction ends."

The Remy was a property I'd had my eye on for the last two years. Bora Bora was one of my favorite places to escape, and over a card game I learned the owners were considering selling. I'd decided to jump at the chance. It was something I would purchase with my own funds, not those belonging to HPZ. My ultimate plan was to take the boutique resort and turn it into a set of private residences, with one section dedicated as my personal retreat.

The fact Hagen and Pierce knew about my interest in the property and had suggested it as the perfect location as the base for the project had annoyed the shit out of me. Henna's contract had driven the price of the resort up by millions.

I would get those assholes back one day.

"If this is your way to stall the project, remember it is millions of HPZ funds you are risking." Henna glared at me and then turned toward the side of the table where Hagen and Pierce sat. "Would either of you come in place of Zack? It appears the two of you have a greater vested interest in seeing this project succeed."

Before either of them could say anything, I spoke. "Neither of them is available. Hagen will be on his honeymoon and Pierce is coaching Christopher's swim team. I'm the only choice."

A shadow of a vein appeared on Henna's forehead, telling me she was about to blow.

She clenched her teeth and then I gritted mine as Collin set a hand on her hand, patting it.

"Fine, Mr. Lykaios. You win. I will send you the logistics of the trip. Just don't expect five-star accommodations. All rooms are allocated and there's a chance you'll have to bunk up with one of the managers." She pushed the papers in my direction and tapped the top.

"I have no problem with that." I picked up my pen and signed my name in all the spots marked with yellow "sign here" tags.

Once I was done, I handed the papers over and watched Henna immediately stand.

"I'll be in contact."

"I look forward to it."

Henna, Collin, and our legal teams cleared the room. Just as I was about to make my own exit, Hagen set a hand on my shoulder.

"Not so fast, asshole. We need to have a chat," Hagen said.

I shifted, causing Hagen to drop his arm.

"I can't. I have to take care of something first. You can hold the ass-chewing until we meet this afternoon."

I ignored the scowls of my brothers and left the conference room.

CHAPTER THREE

Henna

I WALKED into my office a little over two hours after the meeting that should have been straightforward and instead turned into a pissing contest between Zack and me.

Because of him, I'd gone into a meeting with all my casino mangers a bit more hardnosed than usual. Everyone seemed to pick up on my annoyance, had given me a wide berth to say my piece, and hadn't argued.

I even took thirty minutes in the Lykaios Spa's salt room to meditate to calm my irritation with Zack. I could have used an extra fifteen minutes to just relax, but work called.

No other man had ever gotten under my skin as Zack

did. How was it possible to want to punch someone as much as I wanted to fuck him?

I couldn't wait until tonight's girls' night, when I could bitch to Penny and Amelia about their pain-in-the-ass brother-in-law. No, on second thought, I shouldn't say anything. They'd want all the details and I'd end up confessing that Zack and I had slept together.

"Ms. Anthony," Yvette, my personal assistant, said as I approached her desk, "Mr. Lykaios is waiting for you in your office."

I frowned. "How is that possible? Collin is at the natatorium with Pierce watching Christopher's swim practice."

Christopher had brought Pierce and Collin back together in a way nothing could have done before. That little boy made me wish for a child just like him one day, so full of love and kindness.

For that to come true, Henna, you need a man who doesn't make you think of homicide.

"It isn't Mr. Collin. It's Mr. Zacharias Lykaios."

"You let him in my office?"

Yvette was loyal, and for her to do this made no sense.

"No, ma'am. I was in the copy room and when I returned, he was sitting on the sofa in your office. I wasn't sure how I could tactfully ask him to leave without causing a scene."

I sighed. "Don't worry about it, Yvette. Zack is a bulldozer. I'll take care of him."

I strode to my office and pushed open the door.

"What the fuck is your problem and why are you here?"

Zack shifted on the sofa to look in my direction. The impact of his gorgeous face was like being hit by a ton of bricks. He was too damned pretty for his own good.

He remained quiet and studied me from top to bottom. Heat flashed behind his eyes, making my core spasm.

"Is there a problem, Ms. Anthony?" He stood and walked past me, closing the door and then pushing a button on the wall to darken the glass walls of the office.

That simple movement had my heart beating faster.

"Make yourself at home, why don't you." I folded my arms across my chest.

"I think I will."

"What do you want, Zack? You've taken up more of my time than I wanted today already."

"Looks like I'll be taking up some more."

"You are about on my last nerve. All you had to do was sign the fucking papers. If you had issues, you should have brought them up weeks ago. Do you realize how many things I have to rework to accommodate you? The Remy is a small resort with limited occupancy. We're already doubling and tripling up as it is."

"Well, if you're so worried about the space I'll take up, then I can share your room with you."

"The hell you will."

"You can't tell me it's about decorum. I spent the better part of the other evening and early morning inside you. I know what you hide under those tailored suits." His eyes were angry. "You can sneak out every day like a thief in the night if it's too much to face me."

My cheeks heated. I expected his annoyance but not this anger. Then my temper flared. Everything he'd put everyone through at the meeting had to do with what had happened that morning.

"You caused all this trouble because I wasn't there in the morning? Are you fucking kidding me? Aren't you the one who's notorious for never spending the night with a lover? I was just saving you the trouble of kicking me out."

"I wouldn't have kicked you out." His gaze bored into mine. "My plan was to fuck you raw before both of us had to go to work."

His crude words had my core spasming. I turned away and moved toward the windows overlooking the Strip. I couldn't let the visions of what I'd let him do to me cloud what I knew was the truth.

I stared down at the moving cars and pedestrians on the street below and said, "Don't give me that. You have a reputation. I know I'm one of a million women to traipse through your place. Unlike Hagen, you're known for leaving a trail of scorned lovers who like to talk."

"The only woman I have ever brought to my home is you." His tone was hard and almost sounded a little hurt.

"What?" I turned, not believing his words. "That can't be true."

"Did I stutter?" He approached me, making me take a step back.

Why was he so freaking tall? Even with my four-inch heels I barely came up to his shoulder.

He lifted his hand and I held my breath.

Please don't touch me. If you do, I'll want to jump you.

"It was inevitable." He took a lock of my hair and twirled it around his finger.

"What was?"

"Us. The incredible sex. The power plays."

"We have chemistry. That doesn't make me different from any other woman. You're a good-looking man."

A crease formed between his brows, and he moved closer, crowding me against the window. "You aren't just any woman, Henna."

I pushed at his chest to move him back, but he wouldn't budge. Instead, he grabbed my fingers, bringing them to his lips.

"This is a bad idea, Zack. That night should never have happened."

He bit down on my fingertips, sending a rush of arousal to my pussy. "As I said, it was inevitable."

"It's dangerous." Anything with Zack would only lead to heartache. "We're looking for two different things."

"Tell me, what am I looking for?"

"A woman to look good on your arm, warm your bed, and disappear at all other times, not giving you any trouble. I will never be that."

"What if I said I want trouble?"

I rolled my eyes. "And I have a bridge to sell you. Let it go, Zack. Your brother is marrying my cousin. Our families are too entangled."

"We aren't related, and this isn't some Greek mythological family tree."

If he only knew. My mind moved to Anaya, but I immediately pushed the thoughts back. Those were discussions for another day.

"What happened the other night can never happen again."

Before he could respond, Yvette's voice came over the speaker on my phone. "Ms. Anthony, your video conference with Mr. Shah starts in two minutes."

"Let me go." I stared up at Zack. "I have to work. I'll send you the logistics for Bora Bora."

I shifted to slip under Zack's arm, but he caught my waist and leaned toward my face, his breath warm against my skin.

"No matter how much you want to deny it, you and I are going to happen over and over again." He bit my lower lip, rubbing his tongue over the spot to soothe the sting. "Now that I've had a taste of you, I plan to gorge."

"Zack," I murmured as he covered my mouth with his.

He tasted so good, so intoxicating. My nipples hardened to stiff peaks and my desire for this exasperating man grew. He kissed me as if he were consuming his favorite beverage.

This had to stop. I was at work. He was the enemy.

Instead of pushing him away, I was gripping his shirt, pulling him closer. My body ached, wanting nothing more than the feel of Zack's cock deep inside me.

I jerked as Yvette spoke again. "Ms. Anthony. Your meeting."

If I wasn't mistaken, there was humor in her tone, as if she knew exactly what was happening in my office.

Zack stared at me, his lips swollen from our kisses and eyes desire-glazed cobalt.

"This is far from a one-night thing." He released me, stepping back to straighten his clothes, and then left my office.

CHAPTER FOUR

Zack

ABOUT TWENTY MINUTES after leaving a speechless Henna, I entered Ida Astro, the newest of Hagen's restaurants.

I was forty-five minutes late for my weekly meeting with my brothers. They were probably going to hand me my ass, especially since I was known for always being on time and expecting everyone to follow suit.

Punctuality was a must in my world and today I'd broken the rule twice.

Damn Henna. Knowing the sensual woman under the designer suits was going to drive me crazy. I should have listened to logic.

"Good afternoon, Mr. Lykaios," one of the facilities

managers greeted me. He was supervising the maintenance of the grand blown-glass structure that encompassed the length of the front entry ceiling.

I nodded my response and continued to work my way toward the patio where I knew my brothers waited.

The restaurant had a modern, high-end, polished look with splashes of color to offset the ultra-clean lines and angles of the decor.

I remembered the epic fight I'd had with Hagen when he'd drawn up the design of the place. Everything from the fixtures to the menu was designed around Firewater, a whiskey we'd heavily invested in. I'd thought he'd lost his mind when I'd learned it wasn't the whiskey he'd dedicated the project to, but the woman who'd secretly created the spirit. Penny. His Starlight.

Back then a relationship with her was a dream, a fantasy, something he wished for but never thought would happen. Now, in a matter of weeks, he'd marry her.

I couldn't imagine being so whipped that I'd throw millions into something for love.

Henna's face flashed in my mind, and I quickly pushed it back.

Love wasn't something either of us was looking for. We were too driven by our end goals to get sidetracked. The fact we were on opposite sides of the same race was inconvenient. It didn't mean we couldn't fuck like rabbits in the meantime.

"Good of you to show up." Pierce glared at me. "I ordered your usual."

He gestured to the scotch I favored, a twenty-five-year-old Macallan.

"You're late, asshole," Hagen said as he pulled in a drag from his cigar.

"Does Penny know you're smoking those? If I recall, she said she hates when you smell like an ashtray." I pulled out a chair between my brothers.

"I'll brush my teeth and take a shower before she comes home. Now I want to know what the fuck was up your ass at the meeting."

I took a deep sip of my drink, letting the alcohol burn down my throat before I said, "I have no idea what you're talking about. I was only trying to make sure I had a hand in the project as I do with anything we do."

"That's bullshit and you know it. I won't let you fuck this deal up because of your personal vendetta." Pierce glared at me.

"If I recall, destroying Collin was a common goal. It was the driving force behind the creation of HPZ. Just because you two have gone soft doesn't mean I have."

"I repeat. You're an asshole." Hagen leaned back in his chair as a server approached, setting food on the table.

He was right. I was an asshole. It was what had made me successful. I took risks without giving two thoughts to the consequences. I'd lost some but won more than the odds would have said possible.

"I didn't hear you complaining when I won the money for our first project. If I recall, you congratulated me on my balls."

"There's a huge difference between fucking with my family's future and playing poker with mobsters and winning. Don't make an enemy of Henna. She has as powerful connections as you do. And I would almost bet she's worth as much as you are, Mr. Moneybags. She just keeps everything on the down-low. It's better for the world to believe she's riding Collin's charity tail than let them see she isn't the fragile daughter of a criminal." Pierce scowled at me and shook his head.

"What are you saying? Who's she connected to?"

"Sylvia Thanos and Eric Donavon."

Well, fuck. Sylvia Thanos was Pierce's fiancée Amelia's former grandmother-in-law and a power in the Greek business scene, who had no qualms about using force to gain her desired results. And Eric Donavon was an Irish mogul with ties to nearly every underground crime syndicate in Europe.

Why the fuck was she involved with Donavon especially? That's when it hit me.

There were rumors a woman had taken a pot worth over a hundred million from Donavon in a game he'd organized in Monte Carlo. Instead of being pissed, he'd offered the woman a partnership. What type of partnership was still unknown.

Was he a past lover? Donavon was the ultra-polished, elitist type.

The thought of her in Donavon's bed made me clench my teeth.

"She's the mystery woman?" I asked, but knowing it was her.

"Yes." Pierce released a deep breath.

"Why didn't you say something? This game was nearly eight years ago. I could have stopped her. Do you realize how dangerous working with Donavon is?"

Donavon had a reputation for destroying anyone who was on his bad side.

"Get off your high horse. Eight years ago, we were too up to our own necks in Draco Jackson's world to think of anything outside of surviving." Hagen swirled the Firewater whiskey in his tumbler.

Draco Jackson was a local mob boss with ties to the Yakuza, the organized crime syndicate in Japan. He'd moved to Vegas about fifty years ago and created an American version of the world he'd grown up in. Draco also was the man who'd picked Hagen off the streets when Collin had thrown him out at seventeen. He'd given Hagen a job as an enforcer and the means to help Pierce and me as we met the same fate Hagen had experienced at Collin's hand.

If it weren't for Draco, none of us would be here today.

God, I hated Collin. Because of him, our family was destroyed. Because of him, I'd had to enter underground gambling rings to help Hagen support us and get Pierce into rehab after his Olympic career imploded and he'd turned to alcohol to cope. Because of Collin, I wasn't able to spend the final days of my mother's life with her. The last was something I would never forgive the bastard for. He would pay.

"Point taken," I said, then turned to Hagen. "I can assume you were the first to discover this little secret. How did you find out? Was it when you discovered Penny was behind Firewater?"

Penny was the creative genius behind Firewater, an elderflower-infused whiskey she'd created in a lab that tasted as if it were aged for decades instead of a few months. Firewater was currently the most coveted spirit on the market with some bottlings going for thousands of dollars per ounce.

Pierce spoke. "I was the lucky one to learn this information. Last month while we were all in Greece for my engagement party, I overheard Sylvia and Henna laughing and discussing the game as if it was a fond memory." Pierce gulped down his drink. "Amelia thought I was blowing things out of proportion and that Sylvia would never allow any of the girls to get into dangerous situations. She views her grandmother-in-law as a sweet, harmless old lady, even though she knows damn well that Sylvia is her own version of a mob boss."

Hagen shook his head. "These women are going to make us go gray with all their secrets and crazy antics. All I can say is that I'm relieved Anaya is interning for a legit tech company. I wouldn't put it past her to join some underground spy organization for the adventure of it."

"Why would you investigate Anaya's school?" I asked. "I get she's Penny's baby cousin but that's a bit overprotective, even for you."

"Things are different now." Hagen looked over at Pierce, who nodded. "I think you need to finish that scotch. This is going to be hard to hear, but it will put all the pieces together of why this project with Collin and Henna is so important to us."

"Cut the dramatics. What the fuck is going on?"

"I think it's better we go up to Hagen's penthouse to have this discussion." Pierce pushed his chair back.

"I'm fine here."

"Stubborn jackass," Pierce muttered and relaxed back into his seat. "Fine. But if you make a scene, I'm going to lock you in a room with Henna and let her beat the crap out of you with her Louboutin heels."

If Henna was locked in a room with me, I'd have her on her knees deep-throating my cock.

Fuck, why'd I put that image in my head?

"I would love to be a fly on the wall of that room."

Pierce smirked. "Henna is one badass boss bitch, as Amelia likes to call her."

"Whatever. Let's get this over with."

"You want to tell him, or should I?" Hagen asked Pierce.

"You're the one with all the information, so you go ahead."

Hagen nodded, ran a hand through his short hair, and then looked up at me. "Do you remember when Mama went on her extended trip?"

I was so young that long-ago summer, barely eight and oh-so dependent on Mama's kisses and hugs. A smile from her or a touch of her hand on my head calmed me. I was the most confrontational out of Hagen, Pierce, and myself. As the baby, I'd had to assert myself or get run over by my older brothers.

"Yeah. She was on some world vacation or something with her friends. What of it?"

"Mama was in Greece, not traveling. She was pregnant and delivered a baby."

My gaze narrowed. "What are you talking about?"

"Mama was having an affair. A long affair. Don't you remember that was around the time Collin changed?"

"I was all of eight years old. How the fuck am I supposed to remember this?"

"You remember. You just don't want to think about it."

He was right. I'd adored Collin, and at the time, I'd had

no doubt he adored all of us. He worked crazy hours but whenever he was home, he dedicated every minute to us. Then all of a sudden, he'd changed, becoming angry, reclusive, and withdrawn from all of us.

"Mama wouldn't have an affair. It wasn't her nature." I had to defend her, even knowing my brothers would never lie to me about something like this.

"Think back and then tell us it's a lie." Hagen watched me, giving me his get-on-with-it look.

A memory of a man coming to the house prickled the back of my mind from the year before I'd started kindergarten. He was tall, taller than Collin, with the coloring of the Indian subcontinent. He'd visited a lot. Whenever he was around, the nanny would take me to the park or museum. Hagen and Pierce had started school by then and never saw the man. Then when I'd started school, I recognized the smell of the stranger's cologne lingering in the house.

God, it's true.

"You saw him." Pierce leaned forward. "I know you did. You'd get all agitated when you'd hug Mama sometimes and say she smelled funny. You've always been super sensitive to scents."

I rubbed my eyes and shook my head. "Victor Anthony." My stomach rolled.

I knew without a doubt it was him. And that meant... oh fuck.

"Anaya," I whispered. "She's our sister."

"Yes. She was in front of us all this time and we never saw it. Hell, outside of the tanned complexion she got from Anthony, she is an exact replica of Mama."

He was right. Anaya had Mama's facial structure, hazel eyes, and lithe figure. She was so much taller than Henna or her mother.

"Why would Mama give up her own child? It made no sense for Mama to do this. Her children were her life." I felt as if I needed a bottle of whiskey to process everything.

Mama cheated. She'd broken Collin's heart.

Was Collin the victim?

No, he'd made his bed when he threw us out.

"I can't speak to Mama's reasons. All I can go by is Collin's perspective." Hagen took a deep gulp of his whiskey. "According to him, he was at fault for Mama turning to Anthony. Collin said he neglected Mama, and her loneliness allowed Anthony to seduce her and gain access to our family's finances. Around the time of Anthony's indictment, Collin discovered the affair.

"Mama wanted a second chance with Collin but discovered she was pregnant. She knew there was no way to hide the truth behind Anaya's birth so she made the decision to give Anaya to Lena Anthony.

"It turned out to be the best decision for Anaya's safety. It allowed Collin to hide Henna, Anaya, and Lena from those who Victor Anthony swindled. This includes

Draco, who lost tens of millions. Draco wanted one of the girls as payment for their father's crime."

The thought of Henna or Anaya being a pawn in Draco Jackson's game made me sick. He had dealings in everything from arms to the sex trade.

Fuck, this was too much to take in.

"Say something," Hagen prodded.

God, how Greek was it that I was sleeping with the half sister of my half sister?

"Does Henna know?"

Pierce responded, "We're not positive but for all intents and purposes, I'd say yes. She was your same age and she'd have noticed if one day her mom was skinny and the next day showed up with a baby sister."

"I know what you're thinking, and you better keep it together," Hagen said. "The Anthony women are extremely protective of each other. Do not. Let me repeat. *Do not* go storming to Henna demanding answers. Remember her family is as much victims as we are."

"How long have you two known?" I directed the question at Pierce. He was the easiest to read. The man's emotions were all over his face, unlike my eldest brother who held in the smallest inkling that he was human. The only one to crack his calm shell was Penny.

"I found out at the beginning of summer but Hagen's known longer."

"That was months ago. This is bullshit." I pushed back from the table, standing.

"Sit down, Zack." Hagen grabbed my arm and tried to tower over me.

I was his same fucking height so the tactics he used on Pierce had no effect on me. I shook his hand off and let the rage guide my next move. I punched Hagen's jaw, knocking him back and forcing him to cover his face.

"Did you think I was some wimp who couldn't handle the truth? I had a right to know."

Immediately Pierce jumped up, stepping between Hagen and me. "For the love of God. I knew we should have done this in private. Calm the fuck down, asshole. Do you realize there are people inside who can see us?"

Before I could respond, security appeared, looking between all of us, not knowing what to do as we were all their bosses.

Hagen's eyes filled with sadness and the fight instantaneously left me. It was the look he'd given me whenever I'd gotten into self-destructive patterns, from fights at underground poker games or my business dealings with Draco or other underworld players. He had been my anchor in a time he was growing up himself. Hagen was the father to me that Collin should have been.

I rubbed a palm over my face. "This doesn't excuse Collin."

"No, it doesn't," Pierce agreed. "But it gives context to what happened."

"Does this mean the two of you have forgiven him?"

"We're working on it."

"I doubt I'll ever get there." I released a deep breath. "Let's go to the penthouse. I need some of Penny's special reserve to take the edge off and help me digest the cluster that is our lives."

CHAPTER FIVE

Henna

"GET UP," I heard Amelia say the moment I answered the phone.

Amelia Thanos was one of my best friends and the head of Thanos Sports, an international sports promotion and management company. She was also Pierce Lykaios's fiancée and mother to their ten-year-old son.

"No." I tried to blink enough to get my eyes to focus on the clock.

Ten p.m.

"Dammit, Ame. This is my first night I got to bed before midnight in over five months. I've only been asleep for thirty minutes."

For the last two weeks I'd thrown myself into making

the car show a success as well as keeping up with my maid-of-honor duties for Penny's wedding. It had kept me too busy to focus on the night with Zack or the project in Bora Bora that Zack had all but bulldozed his way into.

I knew I'd pushed myself too hard and needed rest. Collin seemed to have picked up on my fatigue and had all but shoved me out the door and ordered me to bed.

I was running on fumes and decided to listen to him instead of arguing as I normally would. Plus, the whales who were in house were longtime friends of Collin's and would prefer his company to mine.

"Do you want to sleep or see me get married?"

Sleep was on the tip of my tongue until I registered what Amelia had just said.

"You're what?" I shot up in bed.

"Getting married in one hour, Vegas style. Get your ass to the address I texted to your phone. Penny and Hagen are on their way as is Zack. I can say Zack's response was on par with yours." She laughed. "You two are two peas in a pod."

"I doubt he had turned in for the night."

"No, he was kissing up to some high rollers from Indonesia."

"How is that the same as me?"

"Because you two are piss and vinegar if anyone disturbs your plans."

"Shut it, Thanos, or I'm not letting you book any more fights in my arena. I am nothing like Zacharias Lykaios."

"It's going to be Lykaios in less than an hour, and I'm booked out for the next ten years. You may scare the shit out of the rest of the world but I know the secret to get on your good side."

"And that is?"

"Three boxes of Sylvia's pastries."

My stomach immediately grumbled. Outside of being the biggest badass boss babe I knew, Sylvia Thanos was a goddess in the kitchen. I swore I gained ten pounds every time I visited her on her private island off the coast of Greece.

"No fair. I'm going to tell her you held my goodies hostage."

"Stop whining and get your ass here."

I slid from the bed. "Fine. Is there a dress code?"

"It's a chapel with Elvis. Wear what you want."

"The pictures are going to be interesting." I laughed. "Meet you in thirty."

"HENNA *MASI,* can I lay my head in your lap? The house is too noisy for me to go to bed." Christopher, Amelia and Pierce's ten-year-old son, approached me as I relaxed on the wraparound terrace of their penthouse.

The wedding was a quick fifteen-minute affair that I still couldn't believe happened.

Spontaneity was not Amelia's forte. She was a meticulous planner and as far as anyone knew, her wedding was supposed to happen over Christmas a few months from now.

Amelia said Christopher was the reason they moved it up. He wanted his mom and dad married for his birthday and so his parents delivered. Now the poor boy was exhausted from staying up way past his bedtime.

"Climb aboard, little man."

He yawned, pulled at the collar of his shirt, and then scooted onto the giant, half-moon-shaped outdoor sofa bed that took up a large section of terrace.

I lifted the blanket I had tucked over my legs and let him get settled before covering his body with the soft material.

I played with his silky thick black hair, a signature trait of any Lykaios male.

"You smell good. Mama says it's because you bamboozled a chemist to create a signature fragrance."

I smiled, remembering Amelia's annoyed reaction when she learned Pavlo Rici, the go-to chemist for high-end perfumes, had agreed to make a scent for me and had refused her.

Amelia had no idea the signature scent was Pavlo's way of thanking me for paying off a debt of nearly two hundred and fifty thousand euros to a private poker club in Monte Carlo funded by Eric Donavon. Eric wasn't someone to ever owe a single penny to. I was one of the few people to ever best him. And because of it, he respected me and had become an ally. He owed me a few favors, but I'd only call on them as a last resort.

God, I hated my father for what he'd done to my family, and here I was, friends with a man with more mob ties than anyone could deem possible.

Thank God I'd never gotten involved with Eric beyond business. He was gorgeous in the tall, chiseled Nordic way of his ancestors and had the style of his Italian heiress mother. Eric had an unsaid open invitation to turn our friendship into more but I never took him up on the offer. Many times, I'd been tempted, but I knew Eric was a player and I couldn't risk getting involved with someone who'd move on in a month.

Zack's face popped into my mind.

I'd sure broken the rules with him. Zack was as bad as Eric, and I'd jumped into bed with him.

It was an itch I'd scratched, and now it was in the past and would remain there.

Liar, liar.

I pushed my thoughts down and focused on Christopher. "Your Mama is jealous. But if you want to give her a present, I can talk to Pavlo to create a scent just for her."

Christopher lifted his head, eyes bright. "Really? You'd do that for me?"

I leaned down and kissed his head. "I'd do anything for you. But you have to keep it a secret. I know Amelia doesn't like surprises—however, this one she'll love."

"I promise not to say a word." He dropped down onto my lap again.

We were silent for a few minutes. The breeze picked up and I inhaled the warm Vegas heat. Most people hated the desert weather of Nevada, but I'd always loved it. There was a peace in the barren land. Well maybe not, Las Vegas—it never slept—but outside of Sin City. I loved the cliffs, the landscape, the solitude.

"Did you have fun tonight?"

"Yep. Mama and Dad officially belong to me." Christopher's eyes drooped.

I smiled. "They were always yours."

"Yes, but now I'm a Lykaios."

His words hit my heart and made me understand the true reason for tonight's spur-of-the-moment wedding.

Christopher was biologically Pierce's son but until this past year Christopher believed Amelia's first husband, Stavros Thanos, was his father.

Now that he knew the truth, he wanted to be like the father and uncles he adored.

"You were always a Lykaios, kid. You're as stubborn and as competitive as the lot of them."

There was no response, and I realized Christopher was out cold.

"I'm not sure if I should be offended or not."

My head whipped up to see Zack standing in the doorway between the outdoor terrace and living room.

"It's the truth." I licked my lips, trying to push down my body's reaction to his presence.

I'd avoided him for two weeks, only interacting with him through email and our personal assistants.

"You're good with him."

"He's an exceptional kid." I brushed the hair on Christopher's forehead.

"You love him as if he were yours."

"He is mine. I've seen nearly every one of his milestones. I can honestly say he was my first love."

I was sixteen when Christopher was born to a scared eighteen-year-old Amelia. As much as I loved the sweet little boy, he'd also been a great deterrent to having sex and probably was the reason I'd waited until I was in my twenties to even think of doing anything more than kiss a guy.

"Did you know he was Pierce's son?" Zack approached and sat down on the sofa to my left, running a hand over Christopher's sleeping head, and then tilted my chin so I looked him in the eye.

"I suspected. Amelia was too head-over-heels in love

with Pierce to cheat on him. And I also knew the lengths Collin would go to protect his family."

For a brief second, Zack's face grew hard, and then it eased. "Do you keep his secrets, then?"

"No. He keeps mine."

Zack opened his mouth to say something, then shut it, took a breath, and spoke. "What about Anaya's?"

What the hell did he mean by that?

I studied him and I knew I looked irritated. "Collin would do anything and everything to protect me and Ana."

"As you would him. You knew why Collin kept Amelia and Pierce apart."

His words were a statement but I answered it as a question. "Yes."

"You're his daughters." There was resignation in his voice.

"Everything he did cost him more than you could ever know." I paused. "He never wanted to hurt any of you. He loves all of you more than you'll ever realize."

"That's neither here nor there. He did hurt us. He did destroy our family. He kept me from my mother until it was too late to do anything but say goodbye."

I wanted to defend Collin, but he'd done all that. Not because he wanted to, but because he'd been forced to. By a man, a mobster who wanted to take Anaya or me as payment for our father's crimes against him.

I kept quiet. This wasn't the time or the place to have the discussion about the lies and truths of the past. Besides, this was a secret no one outside of my family ever discussed.

Hell, even Anaya didn't know the truth. Until she knew, it wasn't right to say anything. It was long past the time she should have been told, but that would require convincing Mom. Mom insisted there was no good in revealing anything to Ana. Sometimes I wondered if it was easier for Mom to leave things where they were than to relive what Papa had done to her, to us, to all those who trusted him.

"What do you want me to say, Zack?"

"I don't know. I want to hate him so much. I want to destroy everything he built to make him pay for all his stupid decisions."

I lifted my chin. "Good thing I'm between you and your end goal. I will do everything in my power to make sure Collin's empire stands and succeeds into the next generation."

Zack's gaze heated, and I felt a tingle deep inside.

He liked it when I faced off against him. Maybe that was why he tried to annoy the shit out of me.

"Stop looking at me like that. It's not appropriate while your nephew is asleep on my lap."

Zack ran his thumb over my bottom lip. "Then I'll assume you're fine with it when Christopher isn't around."

Shifting my face away, I resisted the urge to rub my tongue along the spot Zack had just touched.

"You confuse me. How can you want me knowing I'm the person standing between you and your end goal?"

"I've told you repeatedly, Collin has nothing to do with us."

"There is no us. We had a one-night stand, nothing more."

Barely a second after I finished my sentence, I heard a throat clear.

Leaning against the archway of the terrace stood Penny, arms crossed and a look of fascinated interest on her face.

"Don't mind me. This was getting interesting."

Zack muttered a curse and rose from the sofa. "I'll take Christopher in and put him to bed. You deal with Nosy."

I watched Zack carry Christopher into Pierce and Amelia's penthouse. The man was going to make me crazy. Why would he want me when there was a plethora of women who would jump at the chance to share his bed?

"You can stop eye-fucking him." Penny crawled up onto the cushions of the sofa and leaned against the backrest on my left side, tugging on the blanket until it covered her legs.

"Sure, I'll share my blanket, thanks for asking."

"Stop bitching, Anthony, and start talking."

"About?"

Penny growled. "Maybe start with the fact you slept with Zack."

Well it looked like the big-sister act was about to come out. Penny and I were first cousins who'd grown up more like siblings than the daughters of two sisters. We'd been there for each other through the good times and bad, from the death of Penny's mom to me growing up in hiding because of Papa's crimes.

She never minced words with me and loved me whether she agreed with my decisions or not. She was one of the few people who knew about my success in the underground gambling world. Hell, I was the one who'd taught her how to play poker. We had each other's backs, no matter the consequences.

"I'm waiting."

I sighed. "It was a mistake. It won't happen again."

"From what I overheard, he plans to make it happen over and over again."

"What he wants and what will happen are two different things."

"The odds say you are going to lose that bet." Penny set her head on my shoulder. "Henna, I don't want you to get hurt."

Resting my cheek against Penny's forehead, I said, "I won't, because it was a onetime thing."

My gut told me I was full of shit. I knew if Zack and I

were alone again, we'd fuck like rabbits, in the same way we'd done two weeks ago.

"You aren't a casual-sex girl, Henna. I love Zack—he's family—but he will hurt you."

"This isn't love, Penny. Do you think I'd let myself get into a situation like the one I had with Hunter? I'm not a naive twenty-two-year-old wanting someone to love me anymore."

I hated thinking about Hunter Carson. I'd met him my senior year of college while studying in a remote corner of the school library. Hunter was a visiting speaker for the business school and was looking for a quiet place to read. We'd hit it off and had started a long-distance relationship. I'd thought I was in love and it never dawned on me that he had kept me a secret from his family and his friends.

Penny and Amelia had despised Hunter from the very beginning but I had ignored their concerns. Then right before graduation, I learned through an investigation Penny had conducted that Hunter's family had lost millions to the Ponzi scheme my father had coordinated.

Hunter had orchestrated our whole relationship as a way to get back at my father and to find out if my mother had hidden any of the money. Everything he'd told me had been a lie, and I'd felt like a complete idiot for falling for a smooth talker in a designer suit.

What people had no clue about was the fact that we were essentially left with nothing but the clothes on our backs when the scandal broke. Collin was the reason we never ended up on the streets. He'd used his connections to move us to Arizona and give us new identities. It wasn't until I entered college that I resumed my true identity.

Thank God I'd never divulged my involvement in underground poker games or the money I'd amassed. I wouldn't have put it past Hunter to go after me. After that day, I'd kept my relationships to casual flings, never getting invested or expecting more.

"I'm not referring to Hunter. He used you from the beginning. He and his family were no better than your father." The vehemence in her voice made me love her more than I already did. "I'm talking about the fact Zack won't hesitate to run you over to get to Collin. His need for vengeance supersedes everything else. Revenge is what has kept him going for the last ten years."

I lifted a brow. "This isn't news to me. I'm well aware of what side of the line each of us stands on. I won't deny the sex was the best I've ever had, but it won't happen again."

"Look me in the eye and say that with a straight face." She pointed back and forth between her eyes and mine. "A blind man can see the chemistry between the two of you. It's a wonder you hadn't jumped each other before."

"Whatever. It was a onetime thing. I've quenched my curiosity."

"You love to lie to yourself. Henna." Penny's

expression grew serious. "I know you. Be careful. Zack is so easy to love but twice as hard to keep. Why do you think he has such a trail of women who hate him? He never leads a woman on but somehow each of them thinks they can get the perpetual bachelor to change his ways."

"Have you ever thought he's met his match in me? Marriage and happily ever after aren't something I'm looking for. That dream belongs to Amelia and you."

"Then I guess I have nothing to worry about."

We both grew quiet, staring into the night and the lights of the Vegas Strip below us.

"There's something else I want to talk to you about." Penny lifted her head and studied me.

"Shoot."

"Are you still involved in the private gaming rooms in Monte Carlo?"

"Do you really want to know the answer?"

"It's dangerous to continue your involvement with Eric Donavon."

"As is your relationship with Draco Jackson."

"I'm not in business with him. Outside of being Lana's grandfather and Hagen's former boss, I have no relationship with him."

I furrowed my brow and gave her a blank stare. "And the reason you send him special cases of your whiskey is because he's a sweet old man."

Draco Jackson had taken an interest in Penny while

she was doing her undergraduate degree at Stanford. Penny liked to believe Draco watched out for her because she was the lab partner and friend of Draco's one and only granddaughter, Lana. I never had any such misconception. Everyone and their dog knew my family's history, including the fact Penny was related to Victor Anthony even if it was through his marriage to my mother.

My gut told me Draco set Lana up as Penny's lab partner and then kept a lookout for me and my family when we came out of hiding two years later. For the longest time I hated the man and I never hid it from Penny. I never told her about the sordid connection Draco had to my family or the fact he wanted to take my sister or me as payment for Papa's crimes. I'd promised Mama to keep it a secret, and I hadn't broken my vow.

"I send him whiskey because he is a nice old man who is kind to me."

"A nice old man who just happens to be a mobster."

"And you're in business with a sexy older man who happens to be the financier of most of Europe's mob syndicate."

"I have my reasons."

"Like the fact your close connection to Donavon keeps the fear of God in anyone who even contemplates messing with you, your family, Collin, or your business ventures. Anyone with eyes knows you protect Collin with the same ruthlessness he kept you and Anaya safe as children and kept the truth about Anaya's birth a tightly held secret."

I nearly choked on my spit. "Say that again?"

"You heard me."

"But how did you find out?"

"It's a long story. I just want you to know I understand and that I don't think you have anything to worry about from Draco's end anymore. He isn't the same man he was when the embezzlement happened. He isn't the same man he was a year ago."

"I'll take your word for it." No matter how much Penny wanted to believe Draco was a changed man because of his falling out with Hagen, I couldn't believe... Oh my God. "Penny, does Hagen know that Ana is his sister?"

I held Penny's green gaze.

She nodded.

"Draco told him?"

She nodded again.

"Does that mean Pierce and Zack know?"

"Pierce knows but I'm not sure about Zack. Hagen said he wanted to wait to tell Zack since he was the most affected by their mother's death. I don't think he could handle having Rhea Lykaios knocked off the pedestal he's had her on for his whole life."

I felt as if the blood were rushing from my head. "Please tell Hagen not to tell him. Zack may confront my mom or Ana. I don't want anyone to say anything to Ana. She doesn't know. Mama didn't want her to know."

The panic settling in my stomach had me wishing I'd stayed in bed instead of coming to the wedding.

"You're going to have to tell her sooner rather than later. Hagen is determined to have his sister as part of his life."

"It will have to wait until she comes back from her internship. Please get him to hold off until after your wedding. I need to talk to Mama."

Penny sighed. "Okay."

"What am I going to do, Penny? I've spent my whole life protecting my family. I have to tell Collin that Hagen and Pierce know the truth about Anaya."

"He knows," I heard Amelia say as she stepped onto the terrace.

She still wore the ivory lace gown she'd worn when she married Pierce, but now her long black hair was tied in a loose knot on top of her head instead of cascading down her back.

Amelia slid onto the outdoor sofa bed on my other side and took my hand in hers.

"Both Hagen and Pierce have discussed the past with him. The secrets about Draco are the reason the three men have reconnected."

"You two are supposed to be my people. Why am I the last one to hear about this?" I wasn't sure if I was hurt or pissed—maybe it was both. These were my ride-or-dies, and they'd kept me in the dark.

"The same reason you have held it a secret from us since we were kids." Penny threaded her fingers into my free hand. "You don't have to carry the burden alone anymore. I love your mom—she is the closest reminder to my own mom—but it's not fair for her to hold everyone's secrets while she lives a state away and doesn't have the reminders of the past constantly in her face. It's time for everything to come out."

"I know." I resigned myself to the truth. "I'll talk to Mom when she comes down for the wedding. She has to know what I'm planning and then I'll need your support when I tell Ana."

"You know we're here for you." Penny leaned into me.

"This is so fucked up. I am sleeping with the half brother of my half sister. Could we get any Greeker?"

"Umm. Excuse me." Amelia turned to face me. "I feel like I missed a whole conversation."

Penny laughed. "I'd get comfy. Childhood secrets aren't the only ones our little friend has been keeping."

I winced and said, "I think I need a drink."

CHAPTER SIX

Henna

"IT'S about damn time you finally got here," were the first words I heard as I entered Penny and Hagen's penthouse. I was running late for Penny's bachelorette party because of all the last-minute logistics.

"Ana." I rushed to my baby sister. I kissed her cheeks and hugged her tight. "I missed you so much. What are you doing here? I thought the internship didn't finish until a few days before the wedding."

"I finished my assignment early and Briana let me use her plane to come home."

Briana was one of my dear friends, who happened to be an Italian heiress and socialite. She was also a member of some European spy agency. Which one, I wasn't sure.

All I knew was when she wasn't on assignment, she provided security for Penny, Amelia, or myself. She was an amazing woman.

Plus, the fact she'd taken it upon herself to watch out for Anaya made me love her even more.

I looked over Ana's shoulder. "Where is she?"

"She has some family charity thing in Rome. You know how her family gets if she misses those things."

"I'm sure her family is going to wish she stayed away. Bri loves to get her mom's panties all twisted."

"Briana gave strict orders to send pictures of all the bachelorette fun."

"I'm so happy you're here." I hugged Ana again, and then noticed her dress. "Hey, woman, that's my new dress. I haven't even worn it yet. Plus, it barely covers your crotch."

Ana rolled her eyes. "Not my fault you're so damn short. I didn't have anything worth wearing in my closet, so I scavenged through yours."

"You could have bugged Amelia. You two are almost the same height and shape. I'm sure she had something you could wear that didn't risk showing your goods to the world."

"I'm wearing shorts underneath, just in case." Ana pulled up the hem of her dress and showed me shiny sequined boy shorts in the same color as my dress.

I frowned. "If Mama sees this, she is going to lose it.

Cameras, Ana. Remember, Penny here is a celebrity and so is Amelia. They can't go anywhere without a reporter pointing a camera in their direction."

"That's why we have these." Amelia came in with silk and lace masks in a variety of colors and designs. "No one will know it's us. If anyone sees our group, we'll look like any other group of girls out to celebrate."

I wanted to say there was no way to hide who we were, especially with the VIP treatment I'd set up at all the shows and clubs for the evening.

Penny lifted a glass of Firewater whiskey to her lips, smiling at my annoyance. "For one night, let loose. If you can do it in private, you can do it in public. Plus, no one will know the carefree woman out on the town is the uptight Henna Anthony."

"I really dislike you sometimes." I snatched the mask in the same blue shade as my dress.

"No, you don't." Penny came up to me and kissed my cheek. "You love me to the moon and back. That's why you planned this whole thing."

"I really hope you arranged for a lap dance," Anaya said as she tied her mask. "No bachelorette party in Vegas is complete without one."

Dear Lord, I really hoped none of us got arrested tonight.

HAGEN WAS GOING to kill me.

I watched Penny laughing and slapping the stripper's ass as he straddled her lap and gyrated his pelvis. God, I hoped no one was stupid enough to send pics to any of the brothers. Thank God we'd all decided to wear lacy masks to go with tonight's Mardi Gras-themed show. If anyone in the audience took a video, they'd only see a bunch of girls out for a bachelorette party and wouldn't be able to identify us. The same couldn't be said for Hagen. The man would know his woman anywhere.

I glanced at Amelia—she was hooting and hollering as she egged Penny on from the side of the stage.

Well, fuck, Pierce was going to kick my ass too. The last thing he probably wanted was his new bride onstage at a male review show.

"Why are you hiding here?" Anaya came up behind me as I blocked myself from view with the stage's curtains.

"I think it was a mistake to bring them to a strip show." I shook my head as Amelia strode to the center of the stage, straddled Penny's lap, and ground her body to the stripper's back. "I am in so much shit."

"Oh, come on. It's a bachelorette party. I'd be out there if my contract didn't have a clause about public behavior."

I glanced at her. "Please tell me you really haven't joined some cult."

Anaya rested her head on my shoulder. "Sometimes I think it's one, but it's just a very conservative company that will pay me an insane amount of money to work for them after graduation."

"I'm proud of you. But I'm glad you're home. It sucked not seeing your pretty face every day."

"Back at you." Anaya took my hand and pushed me toward the main stage.

"What are you doing?"

"Making my all-business sister have some fun in public as you promised. Show the world the carefree girl you only let loose with us."

"Have you lost your mind? I made no such promise."

I tried to tug out of her hold but she shoved me into a waiting stripper's arms.

Well, shit. When had she gotten so strong?

"Hello, Boss. Care to dance?" Arnaldo, the head dancer for the show, pulled me toward him.

He was a good-looking twenty-three-year-old with muscles for miles and a smile that would melt hearts.

Just as I was about to decline, Penny shouted my name and said, "It's about damn time you joined the fun."

I sighed.

"You don't want to disappoint your cousin." Arnaldo gestured for a few more dancers to come over.

They surrounded me.

"This isn't appropriate. What will Collin say?" My protest sounded lame even to my ears.

"Come on, Ms. Anthony. You know Mr. Lykaios will

get a laugh out of it. Show us the inner freak we all know is hidden under your fancy designer clothes," another dancer shouted.

"Join the fun." Amelia came toward us. "No one knows it's us onstage with these masks. Please, Henna Benna."

Penny then shouted, "Yes, please, Henna Benna."

I really hated when they did that with my name.

They both gave me pouty faces, and I couldn't help but laugh.

"Fine, but if I find my face on a tabloid, I'm going to kick all of your asses."

CHAPTER SEVEN

Zack

"OH, for the love of all that is holy. I am going to spank her ass until it's bright red." Hagen stormed into the poker room.

Pierce and I looked up from our cards.

"What did your precious Starlight do now?" I asked, hoping I wouldn't have to get up from the table.

The pot held a cool hundred grand. I had a straight flush and was about to wipe Pierce's face into the ground. Pierce had gotten better at the game over the years, but playing against him was like taking candy from a baby.

"Look at this shit and then tell me I'm not justified." Hagen pointed his phone in my and Pierce's direction as he pushed play on the video.

It showed Penny sitting front and center on the stage of the Dirty Nights All Male Review. One of the dancers and Amelia were doing their version of bump and grind against Penny. Amelia had her hand thrown in the air and gripped the dancer's shoulder as if she were riding a cowboy.

Anaya's voice gave a play-by-play commentary to some girl named Briana. Which told me she'd sent the video to the wrong person.

Then the camera panned to Henna, who was a sandwich between two other dancers. One was behind her with his hands on her hips as the other rubbed at her front with his body and then crouched lower until his face was against her pelvis.

Immediately, I felt heat and anger flood my head.

Before I could say anything, Pierce was out of his seat, throwing the chair back. "What the fuck are they thinking? Do they realize how many cameras are on them? Those masks do shit to disguise their faces."

The video turned to Anaya's face. She had a sheen of sweat on her skin and more makeup than I was used to seeing on her face.

God, how had I not seen she was my sister? She looked like a golden-skinned version of Mama.

"Bri, I told you I would be a good girl and still find a way to get the girls to have some real fun. I won't lie—it did help that two of the guys in the show are part of my Poli-Sci 450 class and wanted to win points with the sister of their boss. Speaking of their boss, did you see I even got Henna to let her hair down? Told you she didn't need any alcohol to cut loose. Next time, your ass gets to play bodyguard and I get to dance on tables. Love you. Smooches."

Anaya blew kisses to the screen before the video cut off.

Hagen turned the phone back to him and dialed a number. "Where are they now?" He growled at whatever the response was and ended the call. "Let's go. They left the show and are now on the dance floor of Aphrodite's Garden nightclub."

IT TOOK us a good thirty minutes to make our way into the Cypress, Collin's newest hotel-casino. Security tried to intercept us per Henna's orders. Apparently, she knew Hagen would show up and had created a diversion tactic. Thankfully she'd told her men to step back if Hagen looked as if he was about to tear the place down, which he did.

When we entered Aphrodite's Garden, I couldn't help but be impressed by the nightclub. There was an eclectic nature vibe to the club without looking gaudy. The color scheme was white with splashes of bright colors in the shapes of flowers. It was high end and elegant without being stuffy.

If Hagen didn't look ready to kill, he'd probably appreciate the ambiance and try to steal Henna's designer for one of his future projects.

I was the first to spot the girls and couldn't help but clench my teeth. They all still wore their masks but now danced with club patrons instead of the strippers from the show.

Penny and Amelia had their backs to each other, rubbing their asses together as they danced. Anaya had some oversized oaf bumping and grinding against her...and then there was Henna.

She twirled and glided with Brady Lane, a well-known choreographer to the stars and a regular patron of the club. He had a reputation for his moves with the ladies on as well as off the dance floor. They moved so fluidly that I knew Henna had taken dance lessons. Hell, she'd probably done more than taken a few lessons. The way she followed all of Lane's steps told me she'd studied dance at some point in her life.

When the fuck had she had the time to learn dance?

Lane dipped her and she threw her head back, laughing. When he brought her back up, she was so close to the bastard's face that they could have kissed, and all I could think of was punching his face.

Henna was mine. Whether she wanted to admit it or not.

Not caring that I was there to keep my brothers from causing a riot, I made my way through the crowd.

Lane caught my gaze, lifted a brow, and then tugged Henna closer, whispering something in her ear. She laughed and kissed his cheek. Slowly, Lane stepped back, bowed to Henna, and disappeared into the crowd. Henna continued to dance to the rhythm of the music, eyes closed.

She was so beautiful. She was the total package: looks, intelligence, and heart. Her only flaw was her unquestioning love for Collin.

I worked my way through the crowd until I was right behind Henna. Her perfect round ass rolled to the music and gave me visions of fucking her from behind. This woman was built for a man to lose himself in her.

No, not any man. Me.

I slipped my hands over her waist, making her immediately freeze.

"Zack," she whispered.

She'd known it was me. Had she seen me or had Lane told her?

Her hand covered mine. "What are you doing here?"

"Dancing with you."

She glared at me over her shoulder. "I mean, what are you doing in my club?"

I rubbed my jaw against her neck and felt her shiver.

No matter how much she tried to deny how I affected her, I knew the truth. She wanted me as much as I wanted her.

"I'm keeping Hagen from tearing up the place to find his fiancée. Did Anaya really have to send pictures of the stripper? Hagen just about lost it."

"She did what?" Henna turned in my arms, and the feel and scent of her sweat-dampened body made me want to groan.

My cock was instantaneously hard.

I pulled her close, and as if on cue, the music changed to a sexy hip-hop beat. The DJ at the club was one that Hagen had tried for years to lure away. No amount of money worked. He was loyal to Henna, and in turn, Collin.

Without thinking, Henna wrapped her arms around my neck and began to dance to the beat of the song. She wouldn't be able to say it was the alcohol. I couldn't smell a drop on her breath. Tonight was about Penny, so that meant Henna was essentially working.

I slid a hand from her waist to the plump globe of one ass cheek. I never realized how much of an ass man I was until I saw the perfection of what belonged to Henna.

"I don't think Anaya meant to send the pictures to Hagen—the message was for a girl named Briana. Something about her girl letting off some steam like the mortals of the world."

"This is bad. The dancer had his hands on her—"

"—ass." I finished her words. "I know, and so does Hagen."

"I think Phillip got a bit carried away."

"That is an understatement and hence the reason we're here. At least it wasn't Amelia who was getting a lap dance, or I'm positive Pierce would have found your Phillip and punched the shit out of him."

"Where are they? Penny said she didn't want to leave until at least four in the morning. As her maid of honor, it's my duty to follow through with the plan."

She glanced over my shoulder and then sighed. "Well that plan is a complete bust. I swear Hagen takes possessive to a new level."

I followed the direction of Henna's eyes and shook my head. Hagen had Penny in his arms and was on his way out of the club. Penny didn't seem upset in the least—she just smiled up at my brother and rested her head on his shoulder. Pierce, on the other hand, had a protective arm around Amelia as he scowled at her and gave her some lecture, one I was positive Amelia would completely ignore.

"What can I say? We Lykaios men are a bit over the top when it comes to our women."

"I just don't see you in that category."

I slid my other hand up her back and into her hair, fisting it until her head was tilted back. "You don't know me well enough to make that assessment."

If I had any say, I'd have followed Hagen's lead and taken Henna out of this hormone-infested club and found a room where I'd paddle her ass for letting another man touch her and then fuck her until she couldn't walk straight.

Before Henna, any woman who thought to ever make me jealous was wasting her time. Now here I was with a woman who hadn't a clue as to how she affected me. The fact she saw our one night together as a mistake pissed me off to no end. I planned to remedy that tonight.

"Zack, I look forward to meeting the woman who brings you to your knees. She's going to have to be one formidable lady."

Henna's words had a shot of worry creeping into my system. What the hell was happening to me? This woman was some kind of witch. One minute I wanted to strangle her and the next, all I could think of was getting her naked and tying her to my bed for the rest of our lives.

A new track flowed into the beat of the old, essentially snapping us out of the trance we'd fallen into.

"I should go." She tried to step back but I held her close, tightening my hold in the hair at her nape.

"Finish the dance, then I'll let you go."

She gazed up at me, her breath shallow and skin warm, not just from the dancing but the arousal she couldn't suppress when I touched her.

"Just this dance. I...we can't..."

I cut her off by setting a finger to her plump lips. The ones that had made me go cross-eyed as she'd deep-throated my cock.

"It's a dance, Henna."

"Nothing is just a dance between us."

She had that right.

"Just a dance. It doesn't mean anything."

She knew as well as I did that the words were a lie. But she stepped closer, brushing up against me.

Our bodies moved in unison, rolling and shifting to the erotic rhythm of the Bollywood-infused beat.

God, she was fucking gorgeous—not just looks, which were on par or above any cover model, but the intelligence and sensuality hidden under the surface.

Never had I wanted a woman this much.

I turned her until her back was to my front. She threw her head back, rubbing her juicy ass against my hard-as-stone cock. I pressed my palm against her abdomen, sliding lower until I was a hairsbreadth from her pelvis. Her breath caught, and it took all my will to resist the urge to go lower. There were too many people with cameras around, and Henna's reputation was something she fought daily to maintain.

She lifted her arms, threading her fingers into my hair. She played with the strands before releasing them and moving lower to grip the back of my neck, which made her full tits arch upward. Without thinking, I let my hand glide up over her stomach, between her breasts, until I had her throat captured in the palm of my hand.

I heard the muffled sound of her moan.

Tilting her head to the side, I saw need and arousal on her face.

"Z...zzack."

I bit her lower lip before kissing her. She tasted sweet with a hint of lime, telling me she'd been drinking the mocktails she was known for enjoying.

This woman was like a drug I couldn't get enough of.

We devoured each other as we continued to move to the music.

When we came up for air, I murmured, "Come home with me, Henna. See where this thing goes."

Henna stiffened, as if she realized what was happening between us.

"No. It can't happen again."

She pulled free of my hold, taking two steps away from me, setting her hand over her chest and gasping for air.

She lifted her gaze in my direction. "We're bad for each other. We have too many family ties to complicate things further."

Instead of arguing, I watched her walk away from me and out the back of the club.

CHAPTER EIGHT

Henna

I RUSHED into the club's observation office, trying to get my hormones under control.

Sweat clung to my skin as did the scent of the one man I shouldn't want so desperately.

It was a mistake to let the dance go in the direction it had.

God, I knew better than to kiss him. I lost all rational thought when I was around him.

My body still hummed from the feel of Zack's arms around me and the tingle of his thick black hair under my fingers.

I walked up to the wall of windows overlooking the dance floor. I closed my eyes and rested my forehead against the cool, one-sided viewing glass.

I shouldn't have danced with him. I shouldn't have let the music get to me. I shouldn't want him so damn much.

Why did it have to be Zacharias Lykaios?

I should have learned from the past, but here I was again with a man who could only cause me trouble.

At that moment, the door to the office opened and my skin prickled.

Zack.

This was bad.

"What are you doing in here?" I asked without turning. "This is restricted area."

The lock clicked and my stomach clenched.

"You know why I'm here."

"It was just a dance."

"I doubt anyone who was watching us would believe your sentiment."

I ignored his comment and repeated, "You aren't supposed to be up here."

"I never follow the rules, why start now?"

I closed my eyes for a brief second and tried to think of some way to get away from Zack. Nothing came to mind.

When I opened my lids, my gaze landed on where Penny and Hagen danced.

Well, I guess she'd convinced him to come back. The man was melted butter when it came to his Starlight.

He kissed her forehead and smiled down at her. They

were so lost in each other, the world around them could explode and they wouldn't notice. A pang of envy hit my heart. Hagen loved her so much. It wouldn't matter to him if she had a past. Or if her family was tainted. All he'd care about was if she loved him back.

I felt Zack step behind me, the heat of his body radiating into my skin.

"They're perfect for each other. Just like Pierce and Amelia are."

My focus moved to the corner of the room in the VIP section, where Amelia dangled her feet back and forth while sitting on Pierce's lap and chatted with Anaya. Both their wedding bands shined, reflecting the lights of the club.

"Yes, they are. They deserve their happily ever after."

Zack set a hand on the glass by my head. "Are you looking for the same?"

Why did he have to smell so good?

I wanted to turn into him and sniff but kept myself from following through on the urge.

"That isn't something I'm seeking," I said.

No, that was a lie. Every girl wanted her dream, but sometimes it was better to accept the cards that were dealt than pining for a future that wasn't possible.

"Then what are you seeking, Henna?"

Hell if I knew.

His nearness was messing with my head.

"Those are my secrets."

Zack stepped closer, his erection a brand against my backside.

"I know a secret that you don't want to admit, even to yourself."

"And what is that?"

"You like it when a man fucks you hard, makes you give up control, gives you pleasure in ways you've only read about in your books."

Images filled my mind of Zack tying me to his bed and then teasing my body with a tailor's tracing wheel until I was panting and so aroused, I was sobbing for him to fuck me.

God, I'd let him do so much to me that night. Things I'd never done with anyone else. He'd known what I'd needed, known I needed to surrender my control, to be dominated.

"I know what you're thinking. Does the memory make you wet? Make you ache?"

My heartbeat grew faster as did my breath.

"If only you hadn't snuck out of bed, I would have made you scream your pleasure the moment I woke up."

"It's not going to happen again. It can't happen again."

"Who are you trying to convince?"

Me, I wanted to say.

His fingers slid up my arms, sending goosebumps over my skin.

"Tell me you don't want this." He pulled my hair to the side and kissed my nape.

Without thinking, I angled my neck to give him access to the sensitive skin at the juncture of my throat and shoulder.

He lightly bit down, making my fingers flex and press against the window.

I moaned as my pussy spasmed.

A hand slid over my torso and then upward to cup my breast while pinching the tip in an almost painful hold. Arousal and need ignited, making me want more.

"Will the memory of one night last you?" His other palm moved from the window to the hem of my dress, tugging upward until he reached the silk covering my soaked cleft.

His finger grazed my clit through the damp material, making me gasp. "Zack."

I grasped his hand, stopping him from going further. "We can't."

His tongue licked the shell of my ear a second before he bit the lobe. "We already have. Multiple times, in fact."

God I couldn't think when he did that.

"It can't happen again."

"Tell me that one night was enough for you and I'll call you a liar."

I blew out a deep exhale, trying to focus on the consequences and not his wicked mouth or fingers.

"I won't deny what we know is the truth but that doesn't mean anything can come of this."

"The hell it doesn't." He jerked me around to face him, pressing my back to the glass, and then caged me with his arms. "Collin has nothing to do with what is between us."

"Of course, he does. You want to destroy the very man who saved my life. I will protect him at all costs." I tried to push Zack back, but he captured my hand, drawing it down so I cupped his hard cock. He was long and thick under my palm, making me want to wrap my fingers around his beautiful cock and work his hard length.

Until this man, I'd never thought of a man's dick as beautiful, but Zack's was in a league by itself.

"Do you know that your eyes go almost obsidian when you're angry?" He leaned forward, his lips a fraction of a centimeter from touching mine. "Or when you're aroused?"

I couldn't do this again, no matter how much I wanted to relive that incredible night.

"Let me go, Zack."

He smirked. "You let go of me."

I froze as I realized he no longer held my hand against him. Instead, I'd been rubbing up and down his thick cock of my own volition, doing exactly what I was trying to resist.

Releasing him, I felt my cheeks heat. I closed my eyes and leaned my head back against the glass.

This man was my kryptonite.

Why, oh why had I let it go past the poker table?

Because you wanted for one night to feel what it was like to belong to a man who knew what you needed before you did.

"Look at me and tell me to go. One word and I will leave this room."

I opened my eyes and stared into his piercing blue gaze.

A man shouldn't be this gorgeous. Zack's pupils were dilated, his cheeks flushed, and his breath shallow. He was as aroused as I was.

"Why me?"

Never had a man affected me this way.

"Because you need me. Under all that control, you know I'm the only man strong enough to give you the submission you crave, you fantasize about, you deny yourself."

I swallowed as my throat grew dry.

"So, tell me what you want me to do." He nipped my lower lip, giving it a delicious sting of pain. "Should I go?" He pressed his body to mine. "Or do you want to see how far this rabbit hole goes?"

Before I realized what I was doing, I threaded my fingers into his hair and pulled Zack to me.

His lips covered mine. He tasted of scotch and his own

flavor. He deepened the kiss, rubbing his tongue along mine while rolling his hips against my pelvis.

He was way too good at that.

I pulled away, gasping for air, and murmured, "This doesn't change anything." I pulled his shirt free of his pants. "You're still the enemy."

He captured my hands, pinning them to the window. A crease formed between his brows.

The pressure around my wrists sent a shiver throughout my body. My pussy flooded with need, spasming and desperate for Zack's cock.

"I have never been your enemy. Rival, yes. Enemy, no." He shifted my arms to one of his hands as the other slid up my thigh and cupped my sex. "Christ, you're wet. I have to taste you."

He released my hands and dropped to his knees. In one swift move, he ripped my thong from my body and jerked me toward his mouth, taking a deep lick of my dripping pussy.

Instinctively, I lowered my arms to keep from losing balance and just as fast felt the sting of a slap on my thigh.

I cried out from the shock and couldn't help but moan as the pain morphed into an ache I wanted more of.

"Put them back. You move again and I'll stop."

The demand in his voice mixed with his warm breath against my aching, swollen clit had me returning my arms to their previous position. There was no way I was going to be able to keep myself from touching him.

No man had dared to boss me around, in or out of the bedroom, and now here I was, letting Zacharias Lykaios command me.

This was so fucked up.

As if he was reading my thoughts, he looked up my body and locked his gaze with mine.

"Is there a problem?" He blew on my throbbing sex. "Like I said, tell me to go and it all stops."

"No." I pressed the backs of my hands to the cool glass. "Don't stop."

"As you wish." His mouth descended on my pussy.

First, he licked back and forth, teasing me, barely grazing my clit. Then his wicked tongue circled and flicked the strained bundle of nerves until I was panting and writhing against him.

It took all my will to keep my arms plastered to the window. The light of the club outside the room strobed around us, giving the feeling of being in the middle of the dance floor.

He hummed as he ate at my pussy. His fingers dug into my ass as he drew me forcefully against his questing mouth.

My pussy spasmed and then clenched down, making me arch up.

"Please. Oh please. I'm almost there."

"I know," he murmured, pushing his tongue deep into my core before pulling out. "How do you want to come?"

"What? I thought it was obvious."

He nipped the lips of my folds, giving me a delicious sting and immediately my core quickened, teetering on the verge of going over.

"Say it, Henna. Or I'll leave you hanging. I know what you need. You know what you need. I want the words."

I thrashed as he slid a finger into my trembling channel and curled it upward until he grazed the sensitive patch of nerves deep inside me. A second finger joined the first, pumping in and out.

"Damn you, Zack. Give me the bite of pain I need. I won't be able to come unless you do."

"Was that so hard?" He sucked in my clit, pinching it between his teeth as he pushed a third finger in, stretching me with a wickedly delicious burn.

My body detonated, throwing me over the razor's edge between pain and pleasure. My pussy clamped down on his probing digits, milking them as if they were his cock. I threw my head back and cried out Zack's name.

It wasn't until I started coming down did I realize I was gripping Zack's hair as he continued to lap at my pussy.

I released my hands, but Zack caught them in his. He held my wrists as he wiped his mouth against my thigh and rose. The heat in his eyes had my core clenching again. I looked down to see my arousal glistening on my skin from his fingers.

Why was that so hot? This man made me want things, crave things I shouldn't. Especially dirty, sweaty, kinky things.

"I'm going to fuck you until your eyes cross."

I licked my lips. "I'm okay with that."

He dropped his hold on my arm and brought the fingers covered with my essence to my lips.

"Suck."

I opened my mouth, following his instructions. My flavor burst over my taste buds, spice and sweetness mixed together.

He pulled his fingers free and then rubbed his thumb down my throat. "Do you like?"

Was it okay to say I enjoyed the taste of my own arousal?

I nodded, feeling my face grow hot with a tinge of embarrassment.

"Now do you see why you've haunted me for the last month?"

"Why do you make me admit things like that?"

He sucked my lower lip into his mouth and released it with a pop. "Because under the always poised Henna Sara Anthony, there's a hedonist who needs someone to make her come out and play."

He was right. My few past experiences had been pleasurable but never like what happened with Zack.

It was as if he'd ruined me for any other man with one intense night of pleasure.

Don't go there, Henna.

"Now that you have her, what do you plan to do?"

His fingers slipped to the back of my dress. "I plan to fuck you all night long."

My stomach jumped with excitement. "Ambitious, aren't you?"

Zack slid the zipper of my dress slowly down, taking his time and letting the material part at a snail's pace. "It's not ambition if it's true. And I've proven that I can go all night long. Wouldn't you agree?"

"Yes," I said through an unsteady breath.

"However, right now, I plan to take you fast. You've kept me hard for the last month and I need to take the edge off."

"You went without sex for a month?" I couldn't hide the surprise from my voice.

His hand cupped my throat, irritation etched on his face. "Despite what the public believes, I do not have a parade of women in my bed. The number is grossly inaccurate. Besides, the only woman I've wanted to fuck for a while is you."

I felt a squeeze around my heart. This was sex,

attraction, physical need. If I let myself believe anything more, I was destined for pain.

Stifling my train of thought, I said, "Then what are you waiting for?"

"Absolutely nothing." He covered my lips, drowning me in his intoxicating kisses.

For the next few minutes, we were like two frenzied animals, wanting nothing more than to get each other naked.

I'd never wanted a man this way.

I reached for Zack's belt, but he stayed my fingers. "Tell me you have a condom."

Why did the thought he wasn't prepared for sex at all times make me feel a sense of happiness?

He bit my lower lip, bringing my attention back to his words. "In my purse."

He reached behind him to the table, grabbing my clutch. He rummaged for a second, found the condom, and had himself sheathed the second I freed his beautiful cock.

He lifted me up, pressing my naked back against the window. I wrapped my legs around his waist and gripped his shoulders with my fingers.

"You ready?" he asked, positioning the crown of his giant cock against my soaked opening.

"Of course, I'm ready. Fuck me, Zack."

He drove in hard, making me gasp. "Oh God."

There was no slowly working himself into me as he'd

done the first time we'd been together. He was so much larger than any man I'd been with before, and the blaze in his eyes said he wanted it to hurt, especially since he knew I liked it.

"Christ. You're so tight." He pulled out and slammed back in. "You feel so fucking good."

My pussy stretched around his thick girth with each thrust. He was going slow on purpose, to make me crazy, to make me demand what I needed, to make me beg for the orgasm he controlled.

I pulled at his hair. "Harder. Please, harder."

He changed his pace, driving deep and with the force I needed. I detonated, clamping down on his pistoning cock. My nails dug into his shoulder as I cried out.

"Zack. Oh God. Zack."

"That's it, baby. Keep coming." He pushed his palm between our bodies and found my swollen clit.

He strummed and tormented, keeping me suspended in pleasure, rolling me from one orgasm to another while he pounded my pussy.

Only with this man had I come like this. Just when I was ready for the pleasure to stop, he covered my lips and came hard, his cock growing incredibly thick and long and spasming.

He broke the kiss and stared into my eyes as he worked the last of his orgasm out of him. Then he rested his forehead against mine.

"God, I needed that." He sounded lust-drunk, making me smile.

Zack's cock was still thick inside me, even after coming as hard as he had.

"You're not the only one."

"We're good together."

"Well, when we're naked anyway." I released a breath, trying to get my heartbeat to calm.

"Come home with me."

I closed my eyes for a brief second. If only it were as simple as that. If only there were no consequences to this attraction.

"No. Nothing has changed. You're still the enemy. I won't let you use me to hurt Collin."

Zack stiffened, lifting his head and pulling free of my body. Immediately, I missed the feel of him.

"This has nothing to do with the old man and you know it." Zack jerked off the condom, tying it before throwing it in the nearby trashcan. "When I fuck you, it is about us and no one else."

"There's no way to prove otherwise." I sagged against the steam-covered glass, feeling the sweat on my body cool.

"Dammit, Henna. What do I gain by fucking you?" He ran a frustrated hand through his hair.

He stood before me all pissed off and gloriously naked. He was gorgeous.

"Maybe you thought to learn something about Collin by seducing me."

"For fuck's sake, Henna. There was no seduction needed. We're hot for each other. Always have been." Zack moved to the pile of clothes on the floor, picking up my dress and then handing it to me before shrugging on his clothes. "Let me repeat, this has nothing to do with that bastard."

My temper flared. "Don't ever disrespect Collin in front of me again. You have no idea why he made the choices he did or how he had to pay the price for them."

I stepped into my dress and reached behind me to zip it up, not caring that I had no underwear.

"Is that man always going to be the bone between us?"

"Why does it matter so much? I'm just another girl in the long line of your exploits. Were you looking at me and thinking white picket fences and happily ever after?"

"Henna," he warned, as his tone grew more irritated.

"I didn't think so."

He grasped my upper arms, hauling me closer. "Even if I wanted more, would you pick me over him?"

I glared up at him. "No."

Abruptly, he released me, and I stumbled back.

"There you go. You love Collin so much that you're blind to the fact he's a sadistic asshole. His giving you the love he should have given his sons doesn't absolve him from what he did to me and my brothers."

"He isn't the monster you want to believe he is. The real monsters are in front of your eyes and you're completely blind to them."

"I know exactly the monsters I do business with. Hell, I'm one of them."

Zack turned and walked out the door.

CHAPTER NINE

Henna

"MUMMY, I need to talk to you about something before Ana gets up here."

My mother, Lena Anthony, looked up from the mirror where she was applying the last of her makeup before we went to help Penny finish getting ready for her wedding. My mother was beyond youthful for a woman nearing sixty. Her hair was still a glossy black without the aid of hair color and her skin unmarred by wrinkles. She looked more like my sister than my mother. I only hoped I'd inherited her ability to grow older gracefully.

Mama had flown in from Arizona the day before, and with all of the wedding madness, we hadn't had a moment alone to talk. And I knew it was now or never.

She wasn't going to like it, but it was time. I had no doubt Mama would do the right thing, even if it meant sacrificing her pride. Well I hoped, anyway.

"Is it about Anaya's new job? I know she loved it, but she looks so tired. Plus, I don't think I want her moving to Washington DC. It's such a long way from us."

Earlier in the day Ana had received an official offer to work for the company she'd interned with in Europe after graduation. Her salary would be in the high six figures with an expense account. It almost seemed too good to be true, but then again, Anaya never did anything half-assed. She would have to spend every long break from school with the company in an unpaid capacity going through additional training, but it was a sacrifice she was willing to make.

"No, it's about the past." I felt the weight of dread settle on my shoulders as I moved to the vanity where Mummy stood.

"I've told you this before. The answer is no. I don't want to discuss it again." Her tone was no-nonsense and sharp.

I released a sigh. "Mummy, it's time. Too many people know. If we don't say something to Ana, someone else will."

"What do you mean, people know? Collin wouldn't tell a soul, especially after all he did to protect us."

"There were other people involved. Plus, she looks like her brothers and her birth—"

"You stop right there." Pain was etched across Mama's face as she cut me off. "Don't you dare mention her."

"Mummy, I'm not excusing Rhea, but she was a victim too. Papa took advantage of her."

"I don't want to hear you defend her. She was married and slept with a married man. Her loneliness isn't a just cause to cheat. To save face, Rhea gave up her child. She went back to her perfect world-traveling lifestyle while I had to pick up the pieces of the mess your father left us."

Tears streamed down Mummy's face. I couldn't imagine the pain of all she'd endured at Papa's, the media's, and the government's hands. She'd made a life for us in a state and city where she knew no one, using a name that wasn't hers.

"I'm so sorry, Mummy. I wasn't thinking before I spoke. You're the strongest woman I know. No matter what was thrown at you, you moved forward and lived your life."

She took my hand in hers, giving it a squeeze. "You and I are more alike than you believe."

"If only that was true." I stared into my mother's chocolate eyes. "It's time to free yourself from the burden of all the secrets. You don't need to protect us anymore. Ana can handle it."

"Anaya is about to start a new life. I will not hurt her. I know her brothers will love her but she doesn't deserve to have this burden to carry. There is no good that can come out of her knowing the truth."

"I know. I've known for years."

Mummy and I froze as Ana came into the room.

"Do you think I didn't question where I got my fairer skin or hazel eyes? I don't look like you or Papa." Sadness shadowed her normally bright eyes as tears streamed down her face. "How could you love me knowing what I was? What I represented? He cheated on you and I'm the shame that came from it."

Mama dropped my hand, rushed to Ana, and engulfed her in her arms.

"You are my baby. You were mine from the second they placed you in my arms. If he hadn't done what he had, you wouldn't be here. I'd live through it all over again, if it meant you were mine."

Anaya sobbed. "When will he stop hurting us?"

"He doesn't have the power to hurt us anymore. Don't give it to him." Mummy smoothed Ana's hair and kissed her forehead. "No matter who gave birth to you, you are my child and Henna is your sister. Nothing will ever change this."

I swallowed as my throat burned and I cried silently.

"Her brothers are good men, Mummy." I moved to where my mom and Anaya held each other. "They'll want to get to know Ana. Not just as Penny's cousin, but as a sister."

Ana stared at me. "How do you know this?"

"Penny and Amelia told me the night Ame married Pierce."

"But how do they know? Why wouldn't anyone say anything?" Ana wiped at her cheeks with the back of her hand.

"It doesn't matter how any of them found out," Mama said. "I always knew it would eventually come out. I just hoped it would take longer."

There was a resignation around her that made me realize it wasn't the fear of the public knowing the truth but that she would lose her child, a child not of her blood but heart.

I set a hand on her shoulder. "Mummy, this isn't something to fear. They know what you mean to Anaya. I overheard Hagen say how much he wished his mother was as strong as you were. They respect you."

"Let's take it one step at a time. They don't even know that you told me. Today is about Penny and Hagen." Anaya straightened, releasing her hold on our mother.

The emotions completely disappeared from her whole demeanor. It was as if nothing disturbing had happened. Anaya had always been the sensitive one out of the two of us, but now it seemed like her internship had taught her a new skill.

Before I could make a comment on her dramatic shift,

Adrian Kipos, Penny's twenty-two-year-old brother, walked in.

He was such a contrast to his sister. Penny had inherited the Indian skin tone and model features from Karina Masi, my mother's older sister who passed away when Penny was born. Whereas Adrian had the sharp features of his mother's Nordic heritage. The one feature both siblings shared were their piercing green eyes. It came from my deceased uncle Jacob's Greek side.

The siblings loved each other in the same way Anaya and I did. They would protect and fight for the other through thick or thin.

"Are you ladies ready?" He asked the question to all of us, but his gaze was on Anaya.

He walked up to her and then whispered something in her ear, not caring that Mummy and I watched him.

Anaya frowned. "Nothing."

"I know something's wrong," he said a little louder.

Ana pushed him away and said through clenched teeth, "Would it matter? Don't pretend to care on my account. You made it clear where we stand."

I glanced at my mother, asking silently if she knew what was going on. Mummy lifted her brows and shrugged.

"Dammit, Ana." He grabbed her arm, and in a split second, Ana made some crazy ninja move and had Adrian's hand twisted behind his back.

How the hell had she done that? He was probably double her weight and a good eight inches taller than her.

"Don't touch me. You don't ever get to touch me. You lost the chance. You live your life and I'll do the same with mine."

Adrian gasped out a breath, and I could tell he was letting Anaya keep him in that position. Adrian practiced mixed martial arts every day with a coach from Amelia's training facility.

"Ana, I don't have a choice."

"Bullshit. You're just too scared of the consequences, and I'm done waiting."

Anaya released Adrian and walked past me. "Let's go. We have a bride waiting for her wedding party."

Well, this was getting more twisted by the minute. I was in some weird sex thing with Zack, who happened to be my half sister's half brother, and my half sister was in some unsaid thing with my cousin's half brother.

There was no doubt we were a very tangled family. The Greek Gods would be proud.

Zack

I WALKED into my weekly poker game located in the

middle of a group of warehouses on the outskirts of Vegas, a bit exhausted and suffering from a mild hangover. It had been less than twenty-four hours since Penny and Hagen had said their vows on Henna's fancy estate.

Fancy was an understatement for her house. I'd heard about the estate Henna had built for herself but never expected what we'd driven up to. Now I understood why it had taken two years to build. The place looked quaint, nothing grand from a distance, then when one drove up, they were hit with a sprawling estate that camouflaged into the surrounding desert and canyons.

Whoever Henna had hired to design the house knew her well. It was a homage to her understated elegance. Until someone got to know the woman, they wouldn't see how spectacular she was as a person.

God, I sounded like a lovesick wimp.

But then again, seeing the woman host a wedding for three hundred people and manage to look unfazed by the chaos of the day was beyond impressive.

I hoped to God she felt as run over as I did. I hadn't left until close to three in the morning and her house had still been bustling with people.

I took my usual seat at the table, ordered a drink from the attendant, and then gestured to the banker for my normal buy-in.

Rolling my neck side to side, I tried to shake some of the stiffness from my shoulders.

"You look tired, boy," said Dwight Jones. He was a professional in the poker world, who'd wisely invested his winnings in real estate, turning him into a multimillionaire ten times over. Mr. D, as everyone called Dwight, was probably the crotchetiest no-bullshit man that I'd ever played with. I wasn't even sure I'd ever seen him smile.

On nights when he was at the table, most of the talkative regulars were scarce to be seen. It was a standing rule no chitchat after the cards were dealt. Mr. D had a tendency to punch people who wouldn't shut up.

I'd felt like doing this a time or two but had managed to restrain myself.

"That was an understatement. I'm still trying to recover. Sucks to go back to work after an eventful night."

"I heard your brother got married. Tell him D said good luck."

"Will do."

"How'd it go, seeing the old man in attendance?"

During the day, Collin had tried multiple times to engage in conversation. I hadn't been a dick and outright ignored him but kept our discussions short and impersonal.

"Not bad. My interaction with Collin was minimal. Most of my time was spent trying to keep the groom from wishing he'd eloped. Hagen isn't one for attention, and the fact he had a wedding with three hundred guests is a testament to his love for Penny."

"Never thought I'd see the day the Lykaios brothers

would drop like flies into matrimony. First my boy Pierce and then Hagen. You better watch out. You'll be next."

"Sorry to disappoint. But Zack isn't the marrying type," Henna said as she came up to the table.

She looked fresh as a daisy, make-up flawless, clothes without a wrinkle, and hair in a slick ponytail. My cock jumped as a vision of wrapping my hand around her long tresses and fucking her flashed in my mind.

If people hadn't been still partying in the mansion she referred to as a house, I'd have tried to convince her to let me stay.

"And what type am I?" I stared at her.

"The type of man a girl fucks and knows not to think long term."

"She's got you there, boy." Dwight smacked me on my back. "Henna darlin', when are you going to put me out of my misery and make an honest man out of me?"

"You're too much to handle, Mr. D." Henna shook her head. "Plus, I can't break all your lady friends' hearts by taking you off the market. They may try to kill me in my sleep."

"I'd protect you, if only you'd give me a chance." He clutched his chest as if it were in pain.

Henna leaned over and kissed his forehead. "Let's see how you play tonight and then we'll decide."

Was Mr. D flirting? Hell, his cheeks were all rosy, and he was smiling. What the fuck?

"Aww, Henna darlin', that means you're going to clean me out like last time. Can't you have pity on me and let an old man win once in a while?"

I cleared my throat, stopping the insanity of their conversation. "It looks like it's just the three of us tonight?"

"Let us join," I heard a man say from the doorway of the warehouse.

Fuck. It was Draco Jackson's grandsons, Sota, Ren, and Eiji.

If they were here, that meant Draco wanted something from me. They never sought me out without a favor needed. Yeah, it was always repaid, but it wasn't as if I had a choice whether to help or not. Draco had supported us after the bullshit of our pasts so there was no way of saying no to him. Even with the fact he was the reason my sister had grown up without knowing us.

He was a mobster and behaved as one would expect one to act. Though I had noticed Draco calling on me more often in recent months. It more than likely had to do with Hagen.

In Hagen's youth, he'd worked for Draco as an enforcer doing anything and everything the older man asked without question. According to Hagen, he'd all but cut ties with Draco after learning the truth about our mother and the Anthonys. Hagen had said it would take him a long time before he got over the fact that the pain of our youth was orchestrated by a man he viewed as a surrogate father.

Now, instead of turning to Hagen for "favors," Draco looked in the direction of the other Lykaios brothers, specifically me.

Why the hell Draco had fixated on me over Pierce was beyond me. I was sure I was about to find out my next job in the world of former Yakuza and now Vegas mob syndicate.

As the men took their seats, Henna's relaxed demeanor went rigid as did Dwight's. No one could mistake who the men were, especially in the underground poker world.

The men spoke in Japanese as they settled in and then focused on Henna.

"Ms. Anthony." Sota nodded toward her. "Good to see you."

She inclined her head but said nothing more.

"How is Mr. Donavon? I heard he came to visit."

Henna picked up her drink, stared Sota in the eyes, and said with a smile, "Dangerous."

Well, fuck. They weren't here for me, but for Henna.

"Good to know. *Ojiisan* has nothing but praise for him."

"I'll be sure to pass that along." Henna swirled the amber liquid in her glass.

"Have your mother and sister returned safely to Arizona?"

Henna's gaze narrowed. The last thing to discuss with her was her family. She was a mama bear when it came to protecting them, especially Henna's mother. Lena Anthony had suffered her whole life and needed peace, and her remaining in Vegas would only bring back painful memories.

"Yes. Their security team reported they are settled in at home."

Henna had to stop with the veiled taunts. Sota was only going to humor her so long.

Before I could steer the conversation in another direction, Sota spoke again. "How is the real-estate business?"

What real-estate business? When the hell had Henna gotten into real estate? Then I remembered what Pierce and Hagen had said about Henna having investments beyond poker. Well hell, if she was on Draco's radar outside of his history with her father, then it meant she was a big player.

"As well as can be expected. It is a buyer's market."

"*Ojiisan* says you procured a property he's had his eye on for the last few years."

A calculated smile touched Henna's lips. "It's not procuring if I've owned the land for five years. However, I'm always willing to sell. That is, for the right price."

"I'll have to see if something can be negotiated."

"You know where to find me."

"Yes, we do. Won't you need to get approval from your business partner?"

"You should do better research, Mr. Jackson. Mr. Donavon and I are friends, not partners. I need no one's counsel."

I felt as if I was watching an unspoken conversation and had no idea where to jump in.

What property were they talking about? Then it hit me. Draco had asked me to inquire about a set of small islands in the Caribbean. The original owner had handed it down for three generations until five years ago when it passed to an unknown entity. Rumor had it that it was payment to cover gambling debts incurred over the course of a few years.

Now it made sense—Henna working as Collin's protege was a front for what she was truly doing. She collected debts from high rollers. Which meant Donavon was her muscle.

I almost wanted to shake her. She was playing snake charmer in a tank of vipers.

"If no one else is buying in, let's start the game. I don't have all damn night to wait for the chitchat to stop." Dwight scowled at Draco's grandsons and then turned to the dealer. "Deal us in."

For the next hour, everyone played virtually in silence. Henna's face showed no emotion—it was like a beautiful frozen canvas. I'd seen this look before, and it only meant she was out for the kill tonight.

I could understand her determination to best the Jackson crew.

"Cash me out," Dwight barked. "I feel like I'm at a wake instead of a poker game. Tell your grandfather to teach the three of you to have some fun then maybe we can enjoy your company."

Dwight pushed back from the table and walked toward the banker.

"He has a point, Sota," I couldn't help but add in. "I'd expect the uptight enforcer act from Ren and Eiji but not you."

The glare I got from him reminded me of his grandfather but didn't have the same effect on me. I'd spent too many years with the Jackson crew to be intimidated by anyone but Draco. Well, and his wife. The pair followed the traditional respect structure that was customary in Japanese culture. Any slight to Draco or his beloved *Obaasan* could all but sign one's death warrant.

I may have had a fondness for Draco but I wasn't stupid enough to cross him. It was a fine line my brothers and I straddled. Thankfully, our dealings were on the up-and-up. Well, outside of our underground poker games.

It took another hour of play before Henna seemed to have reached her fill of the Jackson family.

"Before this night goes further, what do you want from me, Mr. Jackson? I know you didn't invite yourself to this game without a reason."

Sota and Ren shared a look, conveying some kind of communication. "*Ojiisan* requests a private meeting with you to discuss the past and any debts owed to him by your father."

"Does he now?" Fire flashed in Henna's gaze. "As far as I see it, the debt owed is to me. When he is ready to pay, then I will meet him. Not a moment before."

"It is in your best interest to meet with him." Eiji spoke for the first time in the evening.

"No, what's best for my interest is for you to stay away from me. I'm not the weak girl your precious *Ojiisan* forced into hiding anymore." She pushed her chair back and rose. "I believe it's better if we called it a night."

"We're not done." Ren grabbed Henna's arm, and out of instinct, I pulled Ren away from her.

"Don't touch her. Never touch her again." Out of the corner of my eye, I saw Henna's security get into position to protect her.

With a sneer, Sota looked between Henna and me and then nodded to Ren, who stepped away from Henna.

"Mr. Lykaios, *Ojiisan* wanted me to inform you that the financing project you've spent the last few years working on is coming along. Should I schedule an appointment with him?"

Henna watched me like a hawk, anger radiating out of her in waves.

Sota brought up my business with Draco on purpose to

emphasize my relationship with his family, to make me an enemy in Henna's eyes. It was also a warning to stay out of their business or they would ruin the plan I'd spent most of my adult life working on. A plan I wasn't so sure was the right thing to enact anymore.

"I see you have pressing business to arrange. Good night." Henna turned and walked out of the room with her head high like a lioness.

CHAPTER TEN

Henna

TWENTY MINUTES after Brandon dropped me off at home, I stared out into the night overlooking the desert. The sun was a good hour from rising, giving me enough time to get my head on straight.

I wouldn't lie to myself and say I wasn't reeling from playing against Draco Jackson's grandsons. I knew they were trying to intimidate me. It was something that had happened in one form or the other for years, especially after that fateful game against Eric when I was barely an adult.

I knew it was dangerous to meet any threats with a challenge, but then again fear had been the cause of my family going into hiding. If there was anything I'd learned from Eric and Sylvia, it was not to blink in the face of my enemies.

And Draco was my enemy.

It didn't matter that he was trying to make amends with the Lykaios brothers, especially Hagen. He may have lost an adopted son, but I'd lost my identity, my ability to be a carefree child, as had Anaya.

I'm sure Zack was going to corner me somewhere and demand why I'd left the way I had. It wasn't like me to leave without cashing out, but then again, I knew the banker would hold my winnings until the next game so there was no chance of me losing my stake.

God, I needed a drink. Something to dull the senses, something to help me sleep. Maybe I should pull out the special bottling of Firewater Penny had given me. Outside of the opening of the new show tomorrow night at the Cypress, I had three days to relax and sleep in before I flew to Bora Bora for the groundbreaking of the resort.

I closed my eyes as the warm breeze picked up.

"You almost look otherworldly with your face up to the sky and your hair blowing around you with the wind."

I whirled around. "How the hell did you get past my guards?"

"They remembered me from the wedding." Zack strolled toward me.

He'd gotten rid of the tie and jacket he'd worn to the

game, rolled up his sleeves, and opened the top two buttons of his shirt.

My mouth went dry. He looked like a walking fantasy.

"Not buying it. My team trusts no one but Penny, Amelia, Ana, and my mom."

"Would you believe me if I said that I snuck in from the desert side?"

I studied his clothes again and saw no evidence of dirt. Besides, I had armed security around all public access points to my property. If he'd attempted such foolishness, he more than likely would have been shot.

Folding my arms over my chest, I said, "Try again."

"Adrian. He owed me a favor."

That was a plausible possibility. Adrian had a way of getting in and out of the most secure areas without detection. But I highly doubted he would help sneak past my security and break into my house. I was, after all, his cousin, in a weird sort of Greek way.

"I'm still not buying it."

"I guess you'll have to just keep wondering. You can't be the only one with all the secrets."

"What secrets about me have you discovered?"

"How about the one where you began an underground gambling ring in college?"

Step.

"Or maybe the one about you entering a multimillion-dollar game in Monte Carlo and beating the best player in house?"

Step.

"Or perhaps that you went into business with the man you beat. A man with ties to all the organized crime syndicates throughout Europe?"

I watched him stalk me, but I held my ground. He would not intimidate me. He wasn't my keeper, or lover, or anything. We fucked a couple of times. It was a lapse in judgment. It wasn't going to happen again.

"I think the best one is the fact you are going head-to-head with Draco and not giving two shits because your muscle is the mob in at least three countries."

I wanted to wince but kept my composure. He had some of the facts right, but not all of them. I never truly worked with any mob organization. Eric and I played high-stakes poker and kept a casual, yet friendly, acquaintance. Well more than an acquaintance, but nothing beyond friendship or business.

"Have nothing to say?"

"I don't answer to you."

"Who do you answer to? Collin?"

"Only when it concerns Lykaios International. Any other time, no one."

"Do you realize you have your life tied up with people who wouldn't think twice about killing you?"

"Just so I'm clear about what you're saying. It's okay for

you to work with the unsavory element of the world for gain, but not for me? Fuck off, Lykaios. You're just jealous I managed it better than you have. I do not now nor have ever needed anyone to tell me how to manage my life."

"Have you thought for one moment that you're putting Anaya in danger? Or Penny or Amelia?"

"There is no danger to them. I've ensured it. Ask your pal Draco. He can't touch the people I love without consequences."

"How have you ensured it?"

"You can't be serious. Think back on all the people in my life. One person in particular taught me everything I know. And it's not someone of the male persuasion."

After a few seconds, he said, "Sylvia."

"Let's give the egocentric jackass a gold star."

The moment Amelia had married her first husband, Stavros Thanos, Sylvia Thanos adopted me as an honorary granddaughter. She'd become a widow in an era where women had no control of their lives. Instead of letting the males of her family take over the shipping empire she'd inherited from her deceased husband, she'd taken the reins, doing what was necessary to succeed. This included making alliances with the unpolished and deadly side of various European societies. Because of her, Thanos Shipping was now a multibillion-dollar company.

Sylvia had seen a kindred spirit in me and had taken me under her wing. If it wasn't for her connections and the loan she'd given me, I'd never have entered the private poker tournament in Monte Carlo or met Eric Donavon. No matter what others may think about her dealings, I respected her more than anyone could imagine.

"Dammit, Henna. She isn't the retired, sweet little eighty-year-old lady you, Amelia, and Penny believe. She is as notorious as Draco. Her ties to the European underworld are an open secret."

"As I stated, who do you think taught me everything I know?" I raised a brow.

"You're dealing with things that could land you in jail." He ran a frustrated hand through his hair.

"I've done nothing close to what you and your brothers have done and still do."

Everyone knew the Lykaios brothers conducted special favors for Draco Jackson whenever he asked.

"It's not the same. We had no choice when we got involved with him. You know as well as I do that you can never cut ties to men like him."

"I have two words for you. Double standard."

"Dammit, Henna, I'm trying to protect you. Didn't you learn anything from the shit you dealt with growing up?"

"Oh, believe me, I learned plenty." My temper flared and I poked a finger into Zack's chest. "I grew up with a price on my head. Everything I've done was to fulfill the vow of never letting anyone take away my power again."

He grabbed my hand, glaring down at me. "Unless you decide to hand it over."

All of a sudden, I felt my skin prickle.

I hated when he did that with his voice. It was like cognac dipped in chocolate, making my core clench.

"We are not discussing sex, Zack."

"So, you admit that you like to give up control during sex." He leaned forward, his lips close to grazing mine.

"I admit nothing." My heart began to drum in my ears.

What the hell was happening? One minute we were arguing about my ties to Sylvia, and the next my body was responding to the slightest inflection of his tone.

"Of course, you won't. It doesn't change the facts. You like it when a man takes over, you like it when he makes you lose yourself in your desire, you like it when you don't have to think, only feel."

I stared into his cobalt eyes, unable to respond.

"Or maybe it isn't just any man, but me. Tell me, Henna. How many men have you let tie you, fuck you, play with you until you were delirious and begging? I bet I'm the only man you couldn't boss around."

"You're an ass."

"An ass who makes you come over and over again." He moved forward, crowding my space and making me step back in retreat.

When I realized what I was doing, I moved forward but it didn't have the same effect on him.

He slipped an arm around my waist, pulling me against him. "Deny it. Tell me the memory of you writhing under me is a figment of my imagination."

The ridge of his cock pressed against my belly caused my blood to heat and my body to feel as if I were on fire.

"Deny that you don't dream of repeating that crazy night in my penthouse." He bit the skin along my jaw. "Of me owning your pleasure, of me waking desires you hadn't a clue existed."

"Zack." My voice was a bare whisper but couldn't hide the desire he roused. "This is a bad idea."

The slight curve of his lips told me he was well aware that I hadn't denied anything he'd said.

I was in deep trouble.

"Yes or no." The heat in his eyes made my sex clench.

Without thinking, I gasped out, "Yes."

That was all it took for Zack to lean down and capture my lips. Fisting my hair, he devoured my mouth, pushing his tongue against mine. It was all-consuming, owning, intoxicating.

God, this man knew how to kiss.

Zack pressed me back against the railing as he rubbed his thick, hard shaft against my cleft. He pulled on my tresses until he had my neck exposed. He licked and bit along my throat, sending sparks of need deep into my pussy.

My breasts swelled and my nipples strained against the confines of my bra. I needed his touch.

"Zack," I gasped. "I need more."

He moved the hand holding my hip, sliding it under my dress and panties. He stroked my soaked pussy, back and forth. I gripped his shoulders as I rolled my hips to get him to give me the relief I felt on the verge of erupting.

"What do you want, baby?"

"I want you to fuck me."

"Oh, I plan to, but first I want anyone out in the desert to hear you scream your pleasure." He plunged two fingers deep into my soaked, dripping pussy.

"Zzzack," I screamed, head thrown back, body arching.

He worked me hard, plunging in and out with deep thrusts. My core quickened and then contracted, clamping around his fingers.

I was almost there.

The second Zack's thumb grazed my clitoral nub, I went over, gasping for air and biting down on his shoulder.

"No muffling it. I want anyone and everyone to know all the ways controlled Henna Anthony was lost in pleasure."

I moaned and rode out my orgasm, too delirious to care that my security or my neighbors might hear me.

By the time I came down, Zack was carrying me inside. The second he set my feet on the ground, he pushed me to my knees. I knew what he wanted and immediately saliva pooled in my mouth.

"I've spent too many nights fantasizing about the wet heat between your lips."

I immediately began to work the belt and buttons of his pants, until his cock sprang free. I gripped his hot, thick, veined flesh, pumping up and down.

The fact we were both fully dressed except for his cock reignited the desire the orgasm from moments earlier had barely quenched.

I circled the rim of his beautiful shaft with my thumb, watching his cock strain and grow harder.

Just as I was about to engulf him in my mouth, he said, "No. Hands behind your back. You get no control tonight."

I stared at him, ready to challenge, but he held my gaze, sending prickles of awareness over my skin.

This wasn't the Zack who was my adversary. This was the Zack who was my lover, my dominant lover. The one who'd taken the control I'd never given to any other man and returned the gift with more pleasure than I'd ever experienced before.

I'd agreed to be his, in this way.

Without responding, I set my hands on the dip between my lower back and bottom, threading my fingers together.

My eyes focused on his tempting, precum-dripping cock. It bobbed, angry and hard, a mere hairsbreadth from my lips. I couldn't help myself. I took a swipe with my tongue. His unique salty-yet-sweet flavor exploded on my taste buds.

Immediately I felt a sting on my scalp as Zack wrapped my long hair around his fist and tugged.

"Did I give you permission to do that?"

"No." I couldn't hide the smirk in my voice.

His grip grew harder and my body prickled with the sensation of the delicious pleasure/pain.

"You know exactly what you get with me. I've never made you believe otherwise. If this doesn't work for you, I'll leave."

"You wouldn't."

"Want to try me?" He gripped his cock with his free hand, rubbing the thick purple head against my lips. "I'd hate it, but I will do it. The one place you'll never be the boss is in the bedroom."

If I was honest with myself, it truly was the one place I never wanted to be in charge. There was something about letting go, letting someone—no, not someone—*Zack* take possession of my pleasure.

"Take me all the way in," Zack said, and before I could open wide, he pushed past my lips and to the back of my throat. "Dear God, Henna," he groaned.

I reflexively swallowed, opening the back of my throat so as not to choke.

I moaned as I slowly worked Zack's smooth-as-silk, steely length with my mouth and tongue.

"Yes, that's it. Fuck, this is so good."

My body reacted to his words and I had to press my legs together as my arousal coated the insides of my thighs.

God, I wanted to touch myself, to give myself some relief.

Zack's hold in my hair became almost too intense.

"Don't even think about it."

I lifted my lashes to find him staring down at me. The blue of his irises almost black with lust.

He began to pump into my mouth, using my hair and his hips to give him the rhythm needed. My eyes watered as each thrust went deeper.

His cock grew harder, swelling. He was at the end of his control.

"Swallow every fucking drop down that beautiful throat of yours."

In the next second, he erupted, holding me down over his cock.

"Fuck. Yes. Henna."

His cum jetted in spurts, almost too much for me to handle. I swallowed and swallowed until he stopped thrusting.

I felt lightheaded, barely able to breathe and throbbing with the need to come again. His desire always seemed to spur mine.

He pulled free of my mouth, wiping at the tears dampening my cheeks.

My gaze went to his cock and couldn't believe what I was seeing. He was still hard.

"Only with you does this happen."

He tucked himself back into his pants before helping me up and holding me against him. He pushed back the sweat-soaked hair from my forehead and then rubbed my swollen lips with his thumb before he kissed me.

"Do you want to go to bed or can you handle more?"

I stared at him. There was something in his eyes. Something that had changed since our first night together.

"If I said bed, would you be fine with it?"

A smile touched his lips. "Absolutely. We've had an eventful few days. I could say you more so, since the whole shindig was here, and you planned most of it." He looked around. "Want to tell me why you need so much space?"

"It was my way to know that I'd accomplished something despite my father's deeds."

"You worry me."

"We're the same, Zack. We will do what we have to in order to reach our goals. Mine is to protect those who sacrificed so much for me and make it so no one can take anything from me."

"Where does that put us?"

"Is there truly an us? An us requires trust."

He frowned. "Are you saying you don't trust me?"

"When it comes to my body, implicitly. However, when it come to my emotions and those I love, not in the least."

"Does everything go back to Collin?"

"As long as you are determined to destroy him, yes. That man isn't perfect, but he isn't the villain you believe. I owe him my life. And so do you."

Zack released me, running a frustrated hand through his hair. "I owe him nothing."

"You know the truth and yet you're going to bury your head in the sand."

"It doesn't diminish what my brothers and I suffered."

"I never said that. I just want to give you a different perspective."

"Fine. I have it. We'll keep whatever this is between us casual, fuck when we get the itch and have things business as usual at all other times."

"I believe it's better if you left the way you came. We are never going to agree, and I won't let myself get dragged into an emotionally exhausting argument."

"Fine." Zack moved to the door and then said over his shoulder, "Just remember, Collin wasn't the hero of my story, he was the villain. And I'm the most like him. Ask anyone."

CHAPTER ELEVEN

Zack

"HOW DOES my dress compare to hers?" asked Natalie Barnett, my date for tonight's sponsor gala in honor of the opening of the newest acrobatic show on the Strip.

She was a beautiful woman who enjoyed the finer things in life and knew how to handle social situations. For some reason, she'd decided to dress in a low-cut gown where all her assets were on display. She hadn't said a single nice thing about anyone since we arrived, and this included people she said were her friends.

She was the daughter of Clive Barnett, a heavy hitter in North American real estate. When he suggested I escort Natalie to the gala, I thought it was a great way to gain a boon with the old man.

Now I regretted even thinking a date with Natalie would pave the way for business. We hadn't even slept together, and she was attached to me like glue.

God, I hoped she didn't think this was a setup for marriage. I'd give up my dream of destroying Collin before marrying this twit.

The last thing I wanted was a clingy debutante with more tits than brains. If she thought tonight would go further than the gala, she was sorely mistaken.

For the last six months, the only woman I wanted to touch, had touched, was Henna. She made me crave her like nothing I'd ever experienced.

Why I couldn't get her out of my mind was beyond me, damned insufferable woman that she was. I hated leaving her last night, but she was right to kick me out. I was a jackass and became even more of one when Collin was mentioned.

Henna expected me to do a one-eighty when it came to Collin when all I'd known for a decade was pain and anger.

Even with our opposite positions on my father, I couldn't stop thinking of or wanting her. It was as if we were two powder kegs that were on the verge of exploding if we got too close. No matter how much she wanted to deny it, this thing between us was far from finished.

The need for her had burrowed under my skin. Day or night, just the mere thought of her had my cock hard.

"Are you ignoring me?" Natalie pouted, snapping me out of my thoughts.

"No, I'm thinking." I grabbed two champagne flutes, handed one to Natalie and drank down the other. "As I told you earlier, tonight is about business."

Natalie sipped her drink, tucked her arm through mine, and leaned in, pressing her breasts to my tuxedo jacket. "I'm sure I can help. After all, I'm Clive Barnett's daughter. I was born to be a great hostess."

It took all my strength not to groan. She was really laying it on thick.

I was a fucking moron for thinking this was a great idea.

At that moment, I caught Pierce looking in my direction and shaking his head. Then he mouthed "idiot" before turning to Amelia, who was chatting with one of the performers from the show.

I nearly swallowed my tongue when I caught sight of Henna coming up behind Amelia.

What the hell was she doing here? From what Penny said when she'd stopped by my office this morning, Henna was taking the next few days off to plan and pack for the resort project in Bora Bora.

She definitely wasn't relaxing at home. But then again, this was the opening of a highly anticipated show in one of her resorts. Henna would never shrug off her duties, no matter what.

God, I hoped she'd had as much of a restless night as I'd had. I could still taste her kisses and feel her mouth on my cock working me in a way that I'd only experienced with her.

If it wasn't for Collin, I'd have spent the night losing myself in Henna. I wanted to understand—no, I understood Henna's love for him. But why couldn't she understand the pain a man I had all but worshiped as a child had inflicted on me?

God, I sounded like a fucking wimp with daddy issues. Maybe I was one.

Henna turned to greet some people who approached, charming them as she'd done Dwight last night.

She wore a strapless black gown in the body-hugging style I knew came from one of her favored designers. Her long black hair was styled in waves reminiscent of old Hollywood. Her neck was bare, and her ears had long black-gemmed earrings that I knew were on loan from Harry Winston, her favorite jeweler.

She was fucking gorgeous. And I wasn't the only one to notice. Nearly every man in the room stopped to appreciate the woman who was as smart as she was beautiful.

The fact she was oblivious to the attention made her more appealing.

As she spoke to some of the gala attendants, she shifted so she could introduce them to some over-polished oaf. He wore what I knew was a custom-tailored suit, and the watch on his wrist was worth well over two hundred grand. He reminded me of someone, but I couldn't figure it out.

Then it hit me.

That was Eric Donavon. Henna had brought a mob financier to the gala as her date? I wanted to shake her. Hadn't she learned from the mistakes of her father?

There was a hint of surprise on Pierce's face before he shook Donavon's hand, then the expression turned to a scowl when Amelia jumped up on tiptoes, hugging and kissing Donavon as if they were long-lost friends.

Fucking hell, these women were really going to make everyone prematurely age.

Henna must have felt my stare and lifted her gaze to me. She looked between Natalie and me before her eyes narrowed, and then she turned to Donavon, who was watching me as well.

Henna said something, drawing his attention to her and making Donavon laugh and kiss her forehead.

I clenched my jaw. Had she jumped from my bed to his?

Fuck, what the hell was wrong with me? She wasn't mine. Damned woman. This whole situation with us was so fucked up.

"They make a striking pair, don't they?" Natalie's arm tightened around mine, telling me she caught my distraction. "Who is that man? He has to be someone

important. Henna Anthony has a reputation for seeking
out men above her station in life."

I glared down at Natalie. "Meaning?"

"She tried to nab steel tycoon Hunter Carson while we
were at UNLV. We weren't friends or anything, but
everyone knew of her and her past. It's a wonder she had
any friends at all. No one with any social standing would
give her the time of day." Natalie shook her head. "Did you
know that she all but threw herself at Hunter? From what I
heard, he tried to ignore her advances, but she wouldn't let
go. Girl is desperate to land a big fish. She should know no
one with pedigree would touch her with a ten-foot pole
after what her father did."

I felt anger prickle my skin. I'd never thought to smack
a woman in my life but this one made me want to throw
her off the nearest cliff.

I knew all about Hunter Carson. He had bragged
during a private poker game at one of my casinos about
how he'd played Henna and then dumped her. He'd acted
as if he was justified in his actions and now it looked like he
had spread a different story in other circles.

What the ass hadn't known was that his slight to
Henna had gotten back to me and my brothers as I was
sure had reached Collin. We may be rivals but never took
kindly to anyone fucking with someone who was part of
our world. As of that poker night, he was banned from all
HPZ and Lykaios properties.

"Natalie, I think it's time to call it a night. We aren't compatible, and your incessant disrespect toward others, especially someone who is part of my inner circle, is getting on my last nerve." I guided her out of the ballroom and into the casino area of the Cypress.

She pulled her hand free and defensively crossed her arms around herself. "What do you mean? Are you referring to Henna Anthony?"

When I kept quiet and stared at her, a flash of rage crossed her face.

"So, it's true. She's your whore. I saw those tabloid pictures of you with that masked woman. I don't have to guess to know it was Henna. I can't believe you'd be so gullible."

What tabloid pictures? Shit, I should have thought of it. The night of Penny's bachelorette party and the dance.

"I'm not gullible, and that's the reason this night is ending before you say something that could destroy my business relationship with your father."

"Oh, it's destroyed. You need Daddy for the project in Canada. I overheard him tell his advisors. One word from me and you're screwed."

"This isn't a tactic to take with me." I nodded to Saul, a member of my security team. "Remember your daddy needs me as much as I need him."

The outrage on Natalie's face told me I was going to get an irate call from her father, but I didn't give a damn.

"Saul, Ms. Barnett is leaving. Please have the car called and take her home."

Saul nodded, offering his arm to Natalie. She ignored it, huffed, and stalked past him toward the front of the casino.

I ran a hand through my hair. I hadn't even slept with her and I'd made an enemy. I had the worst luck with women.

Who was I kidding?

I was an asshole when a woman got attached or wanted more than I was willing to give. I really hated the clingy type. AKA Natalie.

Maybe that was the reason Henna intrigued me so much. She made me come to her instead of falling all over me.

She was so confident and strong, like a tigress who knew her worth.

The shit Natalie said pissed me off to no end. Was this the bullshit Henna had dealt with her whole life?

Victor Anthony was a piece of shit, but his daughters didn't deserve to suffer. It made me want to find Hunter Carson and punch him in the face. Hell, it made me want to get some of my and Draco's men and have them take care of Carson.

I walked back into the party and scanned the room. Collin was now standing with Henna, a protective presence around her. There was honest-to-God admiration in his eyes when he looked at Henna. She was his little girl.

Fuck, I didn't want to think anything good about the man, but he'd done right by Henna and Anaya. He'd saved them when the world was ready to eat them alive.

I worked my way through the crowd until I reached my brothers. Hagen hadn't yet left for his honeymoon, delaying the trip to the Maldives by a few days so Penny could be at the opening of the show. Penny loved stage productions of all types and getting to see a show before anyone else was a perk she couldn't pass up.

"Where are the girls?" I asked, looking for Penny and Amelia.

"Gossiping in the lady's room." Hagen smirked, taking a swallow of his whiskey. "Where's your date?"

"On her way home. I didn't need the investment enough to deal with her for the rest of the night."

Pierce smacked Hagen on the back. "You owe me a hundred dollars. I told you pretty boy was about to toss the dimwit out on her ass."

"I'm glad my dating woes are betting material."

"You are so predictable. The second I saw Barnett's daughter, I knew you were going to say something or do something to get rid of her. Why the fuck you'd agree to taking her out is beyond me. I'd rather endure torture than deal with a socialite." Hagen shook his head. "Thank God for my Starlight."

"Hate to break it to you, but Penny is a socialite, she just chose not to act as one." I turned my attention to Pierce. "Same goes for you. Hell, you married an almost Greek royal. You even have the virtual mobster in-laws to go with it."

Pierce choked on his drink. "Believe me, I know. As my dear grandmother-in-law informed me, I better keep her baby happy or I'd hear from her."

"And then there are her half-Norwegian, half-Italian financiers," I added, referring to Eric Donavon.

"Don't fucking remind me." Pierce sighed. "The sad part is I can't hate the man. Because of his long-established and close relationship with Sylvia, he watches over Ame and Henna like an overprotective brother. It's better to have a man with his reputation on our side than against us."

"So, I heard a rumor." Hagen stepped closer to me.

"Okay," I said. "What did our resident super-sleuth and your brother-in-law find out?"

Adrian Kipos was Penny's baby brother and the one person I could say without a doubt could find out information on anyone or anything at any time. He'd worked for HPZ for years and had become invaluable at keeping us in the know, especially when it came to our business.

"This isn't recon from Adrian. It's about your personal

life." Pierce frowned. "And don't lie to us or I'll punch you in the face."

I lifted a brow. I'd love to see him try. If I was able to knock Hagen, who was built like a tank, to the ground, Pierce would be no problem. "This sounds ominous."

"When did you start seeing Henna?" Hagen looked around, making sure no one around us was listening.

"I'm not."

Pierce growled. "When did you start sleeping with her?"

"Why is this any of your business?"

Hagen stepped toward me as if *he* was ready to punch me. "Because she's family."

"We aren't related," I defended.

"She is half sister to our sister. She *is* related. And on top of it, she's Penny's first cousin and one of Amelia's best friends." Lines formed between Pierce's brows. "I won't let you fuck with her."

"If you make her cry, I swear I will rearrange your face." Hagen glared at me. "She's been through enough with her father's bullshit."

"Have either of you thought that she's fucking with me?"

"Says the man who just booted his date because of something petty."

"I'm not the asshole you think I am."

That was when Henna walked by on Eric Donavon's arm. She hadn't even glanced my way.

"I never thought I'd see the day." Hagen started laughing. "Holy shit. She's making you work for it. I'll be damned."

"What the hell are you talking about?"

"That look." Pierce joined in on Hagen's amusement. "You want her, and she isn't giving you the time of day. I can't wait to tell Amelia."

"Whatever. You two gossip as much as your women do."

"You're just jealous we have women who keep us in the know."

If they only knew how true that was. Amelia and Penny were probably the most loyal women I'd ever met. They would protect their men, even if it meant being hurt.

My brothers deserved their happiness. They'd had the hardest blows when it came to the shit Collin had put us through. I knew in the grand scheme of things I'd gotten off easy.

"I won't deny it."

Surprise crossed their faces.

"Holy fuck, you're in love with her." Pierce smacked me on the back, grinning like he'd discovered some deep, dark secret.

"I'm not. We're just...I don't know what we are, but it's not love."

"Keep telling yourself that. I know a goner when I see one," Hagen said. "I saw it in the mirror not so long ago with my Starlight."

"I can't listen to this bullshit analysis of my emotions. I'm going to find a place far from both of you to watch the show and then head home. I have a trip in less than forty-eight hours to prep for."

CHAPTER TWELVE

Henna

TEN MINUTES before the curtains went up for Collin's newest show at the Cypress, I settled into one of the seats in the private box Collin kept for personal use. I'd agreed to come tonight as a favor to some of the performers who had become friends over drinks every time they visited Vegas.

It sucked to watch the show without a date, but Collin was exhausted from his long day and Eric was on a flight back to Italy for some event he was hosting. I guess I should be used to being alone.

Right now, I wished I'd asked my mom to stay a few extra days after the wedding. She'd have loved the show and then Ana would be here too. I missed Ana so much.

Plus, talking to her would help me get my head on straight about Zack. We'd had barely any time to have a conversation that didn't involve her new job or Penny's wedding. And after Mummy flew in, the thought of any discussion about my sex life was out the window.

Ana was an old soul in a twenty-one-year-old's body. She saw things I missed. I couldn't count the number of times she'd warned me about Hunter. She may have been a freshman in high school, but her Spidey sense knew Hunter was bad news. The best part was when she'd learned about what happened to me, she never said, "I told you so." Though she did insist one day she was going to punch him for breaking my heart.

I had a feeling the moment she learned about whatever this thing was between Zack and me, she'd have plenty to say.

Hell, I had plenty to say about his date. Of all people, he'd brought Natalie Barnett. The bitch had made my life hell while at UNLV. I'd expected animosity from those swindled by my Papa, but not the venom I'd experienced from her, who'd only heard about it.

She'd treated me as if I were trash and let everyone know about it. She also was the most vocal when Hunter started seeing me. The lies she'd spread would have made another person transfer out of the school. But I'd learned over the years I'd lived under my alias that I had to grow a thick skin. No one would have sympathy for me, even though I was a child and innocent when the scandal was discovered.

The way Natalie clung to Zack made me want to claw out her eyes. I knew I had no right to dictate who Zack saw, but I'd have thought he'd have some respect for me and not jump into bed with that over-processed bleached debutante.

I clenched my teeth.

Maybe I should have taken Eric up on his interest in pursuing something beyond our friendship. Then I'd never have slept with Zack.

No, that was an even worse idea. A relationship with Eric would have taken my life in a direction I wasn't sure I could handle. I'd become the woman of a mob boss.

Yeah, it was better we remained friends.

I heard the door to the box open and immediately felt my pulse jump. If he brought that twit in here, I was going to throw both of them off the balcony and not care if it caused a scandal.

Zack stepped into the aisle and took the seat next to me.

"There are seven other seats in the box. You could have picked one of those instead of the one next to me."

"Why would I do that when I'm here for you?"

"This is a private box. Reserved for the executives of Lykaios International. And since you're not one and neither is your date, get out."

"I'm not sleeping with her. I asked her to this event before us. It was a favor to her father."

"Did I ask? And for the record, there is no us."

"There is an us, whether you want to believe it or not." He leaned in toward me. "I should have come solo or convinced you to be my date."

I clenched my teeth. "I don't care."

The lights dimmed and brightened three times, indicating the show was about to start.

"Yes, you do. You don't want to admit it, but Natalie made you jealous."

I turned, glaring at him. "Go fuck that bitch, for all I care. You can go fuck anyone you want. We are not happening again."

"Yes, we are."

"You really make me hate you sometimes."

"But not when I'm making you come."

I was not going to answer him. Though the idea of an orgasm from Zack had my cleft growing damp.

Dammit, Henna, control your hormones.

The lights dimmed, giving the room a low glow, and the orchestra started as the curtains rose.

"You can stay in here as long as you don't talk," I said in the no-nonsense way I handled newbie pit bosses who thought they could intimidate me.

Zack only smirked, leaned back in his chair, and shifted his attention to the stage.

Asshole.

For the next half hour, I lost myself in the world of the performers. Their bright costumes and acrobatics created a highly choreographed symphony of athletics, skill, and grace.

The months of training left the audience gasping and in awe.

This production was well worth the enormous cost I'd had to pay to bring them to the Cypress. Collin hadn't batted an eyelash when I'd brought the idea to him. He actually had seemed annoyed that I'd come to him for approval.

The Lykaios brothers may believe they had the market cornered on the indulgence of Vegas but I had singlehandedly brought this show to the casino as well as opened two new restaurants and a nightclub in the past year.

It was Penny who'd pointed out that what I'd accomplished with Collin's new resort was what it took three men to do.

My skin prickled a second before I felt Zack set his hand over my thigh. I'd thought the high slit of my gown would add to the drama of tonight's theme but now I was thinking maybe I should have worn something less revealing.

Zack began to draw circles with his fingertips. I stifled a gasp and tried to push his hand away as I kept my eyes fixed on the stage.

"What are you doing?" I whispered.

He slid his fingers under the material of my dress, and I trapped his palm between my thighs.

"Be very careful. You don't want to start something you can't finish. The best games are the unpredictable ones."

His fingers flexed, sending a shot of goosebumps over my skin. "Is that a challenge?"

I licked my lips, glancing at the box next to this one. There were three impeccably dressed couples so engrossed in the show, nothing outside of a fire alarm would grab their attention.

Moving my attention toward Zack, my eyes caught his piercing cobalt ones. The intensity of his stare had my sex clenching. This man made me crave things I never knew I wanted.

No, that wasn't true. Zack pushed me to explore the fantasies I'd kept suppressed and refused to examine.

He reached up and ran his thumb over my lower lip. "Don't back down now, Henna. We're the only ones in this box and the only way anyone will know what's happening up here is if you make too much noise."

I remained quiet for a few seconds, staring at him, and then said without thinking, "I'm not the only one who's loud when coming."

"Does this mean you're saying yes?" His palm slid

higher until he reached the soaked material of my underwear, stroking up and down.

My breasts began to swell, and my nipples puckered as the slow ache inside my pussy began to intensify. My nails dug into the leather-covered armrest of my seat.

"That look on your face makes me want to fist your hair and gorge on those beautiful plump lips of yours."

"I want that too." My breath was shallow. "But then the public would think this thing between us is so much more than it is."

A frown marred his face for a split second, before it disappeared. "Does this mean you accept?" He pushed the crotch of my thong to the side and traced the wet seam of my pussy lips, making me realize I'd widened my legs to give him better access.

"Mmm" was all I could get out as he rimmed the swollen entrance of my core.

He pushed in, curling his finger up to graze the sensitive bundle of nerves he was the only one to ever pay attention to. "That's not an answer."

I resisted the urge to throw my head back. "Yes."

I barely got the word out before a second finger joined the first. He slid slowly in and out, teasing me in the way we both knew wouldn't get me to release but keep me on the edge of arousal and orgasm.

His focus moved to the stage, making it seem to anyone who happened to look in our direction that his attention was focused on the stage. However, his measured thrusts continued to work me. There was no way I was going to be able to handle this torture.

"Concede, Henna, and I'll let you come."

His words snapped me out of the trance I hadn't known I'd fallen into.

What was I doing? This was a game, and I was not going to lose.

I moved my hand from the armrest I was gripping and set it over the hard, thick bulge between his legs. I squeezed and heard his sharp intake of breath as his pace faltered.

"Is this for me?" I teased. "Want me to do something about it?"

"What I want would require either your mouth or cunt and neither are an option at this juncture."

"It sounds like *you're* conceding." I moved upward, scoring my nails over the hard ridge of his fabric-covered cock.

When I reached the waist of his tuxedo pants, I unbuttoned the clasp and worked my fingers into his boxers, cupping his hard, steely length.

"Henna." His voice was strangled, making me smile.

"Two can play this game." I fisted his thick cock, rubbing my thumb over the weeping slit at the top.

"Is that right?" He plunged harder into my sopping core, giving me a bite of the pain I loved so much.

I jerked, contracting around him, and then bit my lip to hold in the whimper about to burst free. My legs widened instinctively, giving him better access to my throbbing pussy.

My mind clouded with desire and need. Need to come, to make him come, to cry out the pleasure growing inside me. We worked each other, my hand pumping him as he thrust.

"Tighter," Zack murmured, taking his free hand and wrapping it around mine to guide me with the pressure he wanted.

"Harder," I commanded, fighting to control the moans I was desperate to release, and closed my eyes. "Please, Zack. I'm almost there."

"Me too."

Oh God, how was I going to hold it in? My body was on fire and my heart was beating out of control.

I was there, and I knew my pumping on Zack's beautiful erection had become unsteady.

Just as my orgasm erupted, the audience began to clap and the lights turned on, bringing both Zack and me back to reality.

We stared at each other, inhaling deep, gasping breaths.

"We have to stand up for the applause." Zack pulled free of my aching pussy.

I couldn't talk, only nodded as I released his cock,

wiped my hand on my dress, straightened my skirt, and rose to my feet.

It took Zack a few extra moments to get himself together before he joined me.

We clapped and smiled. Then the show director spoke on the microphone, telling the audience to give me a round of applause. The stage light turned in my direction—not just mine, but Zack's as well.

Fuck. It looked as if Zack and I were together.

"Deny there is an us now," Zack said in a low tone. "Every tabloid is going to pin you as the girl I was making out with on the night of Penny's bachelorette party. And the assumption would be correct."

I ignored him, waving to the audience and then doing a dramatic blowing of kisses to the director. It took a few more moments before the show hall began to empty.

As the door to the box opened, I turned to Zack. "What just happened doesn't mean anything."

He frowned. "If you say that one more time, I'm going to kiss you right here and show everyone who can see us that we are definitely more than friendly rivals."

"Zack, I—"

He cut me off. "Dare me, Henna."

He moved closer to me, making me retreat.

"I can't do this right now. I have to handle the after-party."

"Shouldn't Collin be handling this?"

"No, It's my duty." And then I added without thinking, "He needs the rest. I won't have him getting sick again."

A flash of concern crossed his face. "What do you mean, sick?"

"Why don't you ask him, if you're so worried?" I moved to the door. "He is your father, after all."

Zack

I WATCHED Henna walk out of the performance box without a backward glance.

She'd fucking dismissed me. I was not going to let her bait me. This thing between us was getting ridiculous.

Plus, the fact I had a raging hard-on didn't help the matter. I hadn't meant for things to go as far as they had. I wanted to tease her and leave her hanging. The last thing I expected was to get lost in the sensation of her soft, manicured hands.

Dammit, this was two nights in a row.

I took a last swig of my scotch, setting the glass on a side table, and made my way to the after-party reception area. Collin had sent me invitations to every event at his properties for years, so I knew my name would be on the list.

The entrance to the area was decorated in the nature-

and-birth theme of the show. This was definitely above anything we had at the HPZ properties. I was going to have to talk to Hagen and Pierce about upping our game.

I approached the attendant, gave him my name, and passed into the party room.

I immediately found Henna. She was surrounded by performers and show patrons. The flush on her cheeks hadn't subsided, giving me a sense of satisfaction that she was suffering as much as I was.

Henna lifted her gaze, locking with mine. The desire in her chocolate-brown irises made her eyes look almost obsidian. She licked her lips, reminding me of how she'd worked my cock last night.

If I didn't get inside her by the end of the night, I was going to lose my mind.

She looked down and opened her clutch. In the next second, my phone beeped.

No talking or plans. Just us finishing what we started in the theater. Yes or no?

God, I loved a direct woman.

Yes. I sent my response.

Take the card from the server about to approach you with a drink and meet me in half an hour at room 42300.

I smiled and typed. *Yes, ma'am.*

On cue, a man dressed in the style of the performers but carrying a tray offered me a tumbler with a napkin.

"Thank you."

The server nodded and disappeared into the crowd.

I took a sip of my drink, savoring the taste of the scotch. I shifted the napkin and tucked it into the pocket of my pants, letting the room keycard slip free.

I looked up again and found Henna still watching me.

She'd planned this before I got here. There were too many people around us for her to make this a spontaneous decision.

What the hell was happening? I'd never had a woman twist me into knots like this. I couldn't predict what she was going to do.

Why was I complaining? She was giving me what I'd always wanted. A no-strings, mutually beneficial arrangement without the worry about the future.

I lingered at the party for fifteen minutes and then made my way out, spending the next ten minutes saying farewells to the elite of Vegas.

I took the elevator to the forty-second floor and realized it was the penthouse level, the one with only two suites.

Using the card, I opened the door and walked into one of the most expensive suites in the Cypress. It was floor-to-ceiling luxury, with marble and high-end classically designed furniture. This room was something one would find in the homes of Greek aristocracy, perfectly fitting Henna's personality—polished, elegant, and inviting. There was an aura of money and stylish beauty in the space that was inviting instead of stuffy.

Henna's perfume scented the air, telling me this was the penthouse she'd used while her house was under construction. No, it smelled too much like her to linger from the past. This must be the space where she stayed when working late. She lived an hour away and some days, especially when handling high rollers and celebrities, it was better to stay on property than waste time commuting.

I walked into the main living area and saw the glow of the Vegas Strip shine up from the edge of the half-wall balcony. I walked toward a side table and found a picture frame with a photo of Henna and Anaya leaning their heads on Collin's shoulders. They had their fingers threaded with Collin's and there was pure love in all of their eyes.

A lump formed in the pit of my stomach.

I remembered looking at Collin the same way. He'd been my hero. As I child I couldn't wait to grow up and be like him. Back in the day, I would go as far as saying I favored Collin over Mama. Then everything changed.

Fuck.

I gripped my hair in frustration.

Knowing the truth about the past made me feel like my whole life was a lie.

The penthouse door beeped, and all thoughts of Collin disappeared and were replaced by a carnal need for the woman about to walk in. Setting the picture back on the table, I moved toward the entrance of the penthouse.

Henna stepped inside and leaned against the shut door. We stared at each other. The energy between us was thick and full of lust. My cock was a hard rod against my thigh, dying to get inside her slick, wet cunt.

She'd said no talking, so I waited. Then something shifted, and we walked toward each other. I grabbed her face, kissing her with the pent-up arousal I'd dealt with every day for the last six months.

Henna pulled at my bowtie, freeing the knot, and then worked on the buttons holding my shirt together until it was open except for the portion tucked into my pants.

She moaned and I devoured her mouth. I loved the taste of her. Not to mention that scent she always wore. It was like a pheromone-filled drug that always got me by the balls.

She tugged my shirt free of its confines and then pushed it off my shoulders.

I hissed as she raked her long nails over my chest and shoulders. When she broke our kiss to run her teeth along my neck, I just about lost it, ready to bury myself in her at this moment.

Gripping her waist, I reveled in her enjoyment of touching me, licking me, biting me. Never in my life had I enjoyed an aggressive lover until Henna. She demanded as she gave.

She would never give any of herself unless the man

was strong enough to handle her, dominate her, push her into pleasure she never knew she wanted.

I glided my fingers upward, over her rib cage and breasts to the strapless top of her dress.

In one swift move I tore the dress from her body.

She gasped, and before she could protest my actions, I fisted her hair and plunged my tongue past her lips.

A mewled sound of need rushed past her delicious, plump lips. She rubbed her bare breasts against my chest, her nipples hard, pearl-like peaks.

I gripped her thighs as she wrapped her arms around my neck. We continued to eat at each other.

I carried her toward the terrace balcony, pushing the glass door open and then stepping into the Vegas night heat.

When we reach the padded half-wall railing of the terrace, I slid her down my body. There was a hint of confusion before her eyes grew wide. She glanced around, seeing the other tall towers of nearby hotels and realized the possibility of others getting a peek.

I didn't let her take too long thinking, losing the arousal coursing through her beautiful body. I turned her, pushing her against the wall. She gasped as the stone touched her sensitive skin. Taking her hands, I pulled them behind her and then reached for the loose tie that was somehow still around my neck. I bound her wrists at the hollow of her low back.

God, she was fucking gorgeous. The golden tone of her skin flushed with desire, her long black hair tumbling all around her, and that ass, round, juicy, and firm, meant for squeezing, for fucking.

She glanced over her perfect shoulder, and I almost groaned. She looked like a sensual model from a kink photo shoot.

I stroked my fingers down her spine, over the palms of her hands, and glided them along the slit between her cheeks. Goosebumps shot over her skin.

"Zack." Her voice was breathy, filled with desire and need.

My cock grew harder, weeping with precum.

"Shh. You said no talking."

I pulled her hair over one shoulder and kissed her neck before giving her a light nip of my teeth. She shivered, angling her head to the side and telling me she wanted more.

Turning her to face me, I held on to her as I leaned in, capturing the tight bud of one nipple with my teeth. I sucked, circled, and laved first one breast and then moved to the other, bringing out soft mewled cries from her lips.

I cupped her face, biting her lower lip before kissing her in soft, tasting pecks.

"Do you even realize how fucking beautiful you are? You are a walking dream come true."

Vulnerability flashed in her eyes. "You don't need to seduce me, Zack. I'm a sure thing."

"Every woman needs to be seduced." I shifted her again until she was facing the city around us. "Even when she is being fucked, she needs to know her needs come first." I pushed her forward until her breasts pressed against the fabric covering the railing as I pulled the condom from my back pocket, freed my cock, and sheathed myself. "And especially when she lets her lover take possession of her body."

I gripped her soaked thong, snapping the delicate lace with one sharp tug, and then positioned my cock, surging forward.

"Christ," I growled. She was like a fist gipping my erection. It was heaven and hell, all rolled in one, and I never wanted it to stop. "You always feel incredible."

I rolled my hips, working my cock in shallow thrusts, feeling her pussy grow slicker and slicker.

Henna gasped and then pushed back against me. "Zack. Fuck me hard. Like we should have last night."

"As you wish." I took her bound arms in my hands, causing her back to arch, and began to thrust in and out as she demanded.

I pummeled her swollen, weeping pussy, not relenting on the pace until I felt the first tremors of her vaginal walls. Then I slowed the tempo, giving her hard, timed thrusts. It took less than four strokes for her beautiful cunt to clamp down on me.

"Oh God, oh God, oh God." Henna threw back her head, lost in her orgasm.

She milked my cock, clenching and contracting.

Just as her release began to ebb, I pulled her up, trapping her arms between our bodies and sliding my hand up her body until I cupped her throat. I gave her a light squeeze as I continued to ride in and out of her trembling pussy.

Her cunt immediately responded to the pleasure/pain, gripping my cock so hard that I lost all control and came, hotter and more intense than I'd ever experienced before.

"Henna. You're fucking mine."

CHAPTER THIRTEEN

Henna

"MS. ANTHONY, please take the next few hours to settle in. Ms. Steel will meet you for dinner at six," Sebastian, Charlie Steel's executive assistant, said as he guided me into my bungalow at the Remy Bora Bora.

"Thank you. Please let Charlie know there's no rush. I know she's working on getting everything ready for the groundbreaking."

"She's spent the last few weeks preparing. Tonight, she gets to relax with a friend."

I smiled, said my farewell, and then walked onto the giant covered deck of the bungalow.

I took in the breathtaking view, losing myself in the

incredible beauty of the lush vegetation and the striking blue of the water all around me.

I'd arrived on the island of Bora Bora a little after three and was in desperate need of a nap. Even though there was only a three-hour time difference between Nevada and Bora Bora, I was exhausted.

Yawning, I sat down on the wooden edge of the deck and dangled my feet off the end.

Maybe this wasn't jet lag but my body was still trying to recover from my incredible night with Zack two nights before.

Something had shifted with us, as if we'd stepped over an invisible barrier. In between marathon rounds of sex, we'd actually talked about fun things that had nothing to do with work or Collin. It had surprised me how much we truly had in common, from our enjoyment of super-sour candy to our love of the outdoors.

I'd discovered he and a few of his friends had hiked "The Subway" at Zion National Park during the same summer I'd braved the rugged terrain with Anaya. Zack and I loved the feel of peace and regeneration when out in the solitude of nature. Maybe it had to do with the fact we were constantly surrounded by the noise and hustle of Las Vegas with everyone around us wanting our attention.

He understood the serenity and accomplishment of braving the natural elements.

We'd also discussed our affinity for gambling. We'd

both started playing at local games during our freshman years of college, and by the end of our first semesters, we'd fallen into organizing underground gaming events.

Now here I was wondering why he'd left before dawn with a note saying he had to think and needed space. I couldn't figure out if the intimacy we'd shared throughout the night was too much for him or if it was his way of getting back at me for leaving after our first time together.

I knew I'd spent so much time telling him and essentially myself there was no future for us, but now my mind was a jumble of confusing emotions.

Zack was a player. I'd known it from the beginning. He ran whenever anyone tried to get close. So why was he pursuing me? I'd assumed he'd give up when I'd left that first night, but he hadn't. Now I was on the verge of falling for a man I knew would hurt me.

Who was I kidding? I was pretty much there.

As if trying to push me out of my thoughts, a beautiful crimson-colored bird flew over my head and landed on the edge of the plank next to me.

"Is this your way of saying I'm treading in waters I should avoid?" I asked the blood-red bird I could only assume was the crimson-backed tanager. A bird that wasn't native to French Polynesia but brought over by settlers from South America.

Instead of answering me, the little creature pooped and flew off.

Well if that wasn't a bad omen, I wasn't sure what was.

Pushing myself to standing, I went inside for a nap.

FIFTEEN MINUTES BEFORE SIX, I made my way to the main restaurant of the Remy. Upon waking from my nap, I'd reviewed the plans for the next day, from which members of the press were invited to where everyone would stand, which included Zack. I was sure Charlie was going to have plenty to say about the addition of Zack and the photo op he wanted. She'd kept tight-lipped for the last month or so, just saying she'd handle the changes to the schedule. But I knew I'd get an earful when we were alone together. She hated when anyone messed with her plans and an official, public groundbreaking interfered with her work and timeline.

I entered the community area of the property and took in the relaxed yet posh atmosphere, even with all the project crew milling around in work clothes and non-vacation wear. I'd chosen to wear a long, comfortable sleeveless dress customarily seen on the island. Even if I wasn't here to relax, there wasn't anything wrong with pretending with my clothes.

I approached the hostess for the restaurant. "Ms. Steel. She's expecting me."

"Ms. Anthony, I'm sorry to say Ms. Steel is delayed at the job site."

I wasn't surprised. If something was on Charlie's mind she'd work obsessively until she powered through it.

"No worries. I'm fine with dining alone."

The hostess smiled. "This way, Ms. Anthony."

Just as I turned to follow her, I heard a distant cultured, not-quite-British-tinged voice say, "How about dinner with your much older but handsome cousin who happens to be in the neighborhood?"

"Jai." I couldn't hide the pleasure I felt at seeing him. "Oh my God, I can't believe you're here."

I jumped into his arms, hugging him tight.

Jai was the son of my mom's deceased brother, Vinod. We rarely saw each other because of our busy schedules and the fact we lived in countries across the world from each other. Jai had inherited the import/export company my maternal grandfather had owned in India. He was nearly fifteen years my senior and had seen firsthand the hell my family had suffered. He'd been instrumental in helping Collin hide us and keeping the paper trail concerning our whereabouts concealed.

Everyone on my father's side pretended we never existed, especially since they believed marrying my mother, who was a Gujarati Indian and not Tamil, had brought dishonor on the family and was the reason my Papa had committed the crimes he had.

When Jai set me down, I couldn't help but feel like a little girl who was beyond ecstatic to see her big brother. "How did you know I was here?"

"I heard about the groundbreaking and had to see if it was true for myself."

I pursed my lips. "Penny told you when you called her to grovel for her forgiveness for missing her wedding."

"I never grovel. All it took was pictures of the twins from their newborn photo shoot."

"You play dirty." I smiled. I hadn't yet met his sweet babies who'd decided to make an appearance two months earlier than their due date.

"When dealing with any of my baby cousins, I do what I must. Besides, I could have heard it from you, but you tend to keep things tight to the chest."

I shrugged. I couldn't argue against his point. It was the truth. I loved my family but tended to do things alone. Not to keep them from knowing, but to protect them.

"Just so you know, I learned about it before talking to Penny. All the business journals are talking about it. You have to admit, it's a big deal, especially with the history of Lykaios International and HPZ."

"Believe me, I know." I tucked my arm into his and let him lead me to the place where the hostess was waiting for us. "Want to know a secret? It's something no one knows outside of Collin. This way you can feel extra special."

"You can be a serious brat sometimes." He shook his

head as we both sat. "Go ahead. This must be really good if you haven't told anyone."

"It's my company that's financing the project."

Jai narrowed his eyes and when he spoke, it was in our family's native language of Gujarati. *"Is this funded by past winnings or funds you procured recently?"*

"God, you sound like a dad."

"Henna, I thought we talked about the high-stakes games. You promised no more underground poker."

"No, I promised no more high-stakes underground poker. Now when I play it's for fun, not because I need the cash."

Jai crossed his arms, leaning back in his chair. *"Henna, you stopped needing money that crazy night when you were nineteen, so don't give me that bullshit. You like the thrill of beating assholes who doubt your abilities."*

That night so long ago when I'd beaten Eric at poker, I'd had no idea the pot had gone over a hundred million. That kind of money wasn't even a thought in my mind. And it hadn't crossed my mind to wonder why I was the only one at the game in jeans and a T-shirt when everyone else was dressed to the nines.

I wasn't sure what I would have done if Sylvia hadn't been there and made me call Jai, who'd flown to France and helped me funnel the money into as many legal means as possible.

"What can I say? I'm good at the game."

"That's true when it comes to poker, but what about blackjack? Does your pal Eric know you have a photographic memory and can count cards without trying?"

"Only you, Sylvia, and Ana know. That is how it will remain. I haven't played blackjack in years. Hell, I don't play it because I was scared I'd get caught. Besides, the high I get from playing poker can't be beat."

"You make me want to strangle you. You are so stubborn."

"Yeah, well, it's a family trait."

"Henna."

"The truth is that I haven't lied to you. The money for the backing of the project came from all the investments we made from my first big win. I plan to approach Collin about a fifty percent buyout of Lykaios International in the next year or so. This way he won't have to seek out any more outside financing for his projects and can keep the company at the top of the market. I owe it to Collin to preserve his legacy even if his sons don't want any part of it."

I thought of Zack and his hate for the man who lived with a broken heart. The man who seemed so tired at times that I worried something would happen to him.

"I heard one son in particular has piqued your interest."

"Man, you listen to a lot of rumors."

"It's not rumors when there are tabloid images of the two of you at a nightclub kissing and then at the opening *night of one of your shows. He's not good for you. You need a man who will treat you like a queen."*

"You worry too much. I know what I'm getting into. I learned that lesson long ago with Hunter."

At least I hoped I had.

"I live in India and I can see the truth. You're in love with him."

I stared at Jai, ready to deny it, but a hand settled on my shoulder.

"Am I disturbing something?"

CHAPTER FOURTEEN

Henna

I KICKED off my shoes and threw my purse on the entry table as I stalked into my bungalow.

I couldn't believe Zack had the nerve to act like a jealous boyfriend. I'd heard him say he wasn't boyfriend material. Well, maybe not those exact words, but it was implied.

I was so pissed I could feel the throbbing of the veins on my temples.

Zack was lucky he'd only disturbed a dinner with Jai. If it had been an investor I'd spent time courting and he fucked up the deal with his antics, I'd have happily shoved his balls down his throat.

He'd all but treated Jai as if he was interrogating him.

When, in fact, it should have been the other way around. I knew Jai thought it hilarious and kept making comments about how well he knew me and then went into details of the many trips we'd taken together. The stories he weaved made it sound like we were lovers instead of family.

Though I had to say the looks of confusion, annoyance, and then shame that passed over Zack's face when he learned Jai was my first cousin and not a former boyfriend were priceless.

What got my panties all twisted was when Jai suggested Zack and he have a few drinks and hang out. At that point, I threw up my hands and left.

Idiots. Men were idiots.

I pushed the straps of my dress off my shoulders, stepping out of it. A swim in the cool water was in order. I walked into my closet and slipped on my red bikini. I needed to let off steam, and a hard swim back and forth from the dock about one hundred feet away from my overwater bungalow would relieve my anger.

Hopefully the horse's ass would stay at the bar and leave me alone. Charlie had given up her room next to mine to accommodate Zack, and the last thing I wanted to do was bump into him while swimming.

The door of the adjacent bungalow slammed shut.

Well, shit. No luck there.

That was when it came to me. A plan to pay him back

for leaving me alone after our beautiful night together and then for hijacking my dinner.

We shared the same terrace with only a small partition separating his private area from mine.

Grabbing a towel, my phone, and Bluetooth speakers the resort had for guest use, I padded my way onto the deck and set everything on the table near my favorite hammock. After I picked and started the most dirty, raunchy audiobook from my current listening repertoire, I slipped onto the braided hammock attached in a corner.

I leaned back and closed my eyes, letting the voices of the narrators take me to that aroused space I would get to whenever I listened to any book by the author.

There was no way Zack couldn't hear the words from the speaker. As the scene began to lead to the couple entering a closet, my mind drifted to what had happened in the offices of the club.

My core began to pulse and my breasts swelled. I pulled the material of my top down and cupped my breast, imagining it was the way Zack squeezed them as he pinched the tips, the way he would bite my nipple before sucking it into his mouth. One of my hands drifted down my stomach, and I untied my bikini bottom. I slid my fingers between my folds and grazed my aching clit. I gasped and moaned as I began to strum the sensitive bundle of nerves.

I let my mind tune out the book and fill with all the

things I'd done with Zack. The way he'd touched me, kissed me, controlled my body. My skin and body heated further.

My fingers were slick with my need. My core spasmed, and I lifted my hips against the friction of my hand. I arched my head back and squeezed my eyes tightly shut.

"Oh God. Oh God. Oh God," I cried out into the night.

Zack

THE LAST THING I expected when I'd come into my room was to hear the sounds of one of the audio romance novels Henna was notorious for listening to. I knew I'd fucked up by letting my jealousy get the best of me and planned to apologize. That was until I heard the book.

People accused men of watching too much porn—well, this woman listened to the same damn thing.

I'd stepped onto my deck to tell her to turn the fucking book down, but, as I looked past the partition, I found myself transfixed by the goddess in the hammock.

Her eyes were clamped closed as she pinched the nipple of one breast and the other hand worked her pussy. Her pussy was dripping with her arousal, making me lick my lips and want a taste of her delicious honey.

My dick grew thick against the inside of my thigh. I wanted nothing more than to bury myself hard and deep inside her.

I'd taken her every which way a man could possibly take a woman the other night and wanted more.

I hadn't planned to leave her with a note, but there were things I had to think through. Like my plans to take over Lykaios International and throw Collin out on his ass.

When I'd left Henna, I'd driven straight to the club Draco used as the headquarters of his operations. The old man hadn't been there, and when I tried to arrange a time to meet, his grandsons took great pleasure in telling me *Ojiisan* would call me when it was convenient for him.

I should have figured Sota was pissed at me for stepping between him and Henna. If given the option to do it again, I'd add in a punch to the face for touching her.

"Oh yes," Henna moaned, snapping me out of my thoughts and bringing me back to what was playing out in front of me.

I shouldn't have left her. I should have woken her with a thrust deep into her pussy and then pushed her onto all fours and taken her ass. Something I was surprised to learn she enjoyed as much as I had when I'd fucked her tight rosette earlier in the evening.

I rubbed my cock through my pants. I wanted to walk over to her, spread those legs and bury myself in her slick heat. The woman was a man's walking, talking wet dream with a brain to match her looks.

Her lips parted, giving me visions of them wrapped around the fat head of my shaft.

I sat down on my deck chair, making sure I stayed in the shadows. I opened my pants and freed my dick. Gripping the base, I stroked up to the tip, and using my dripping precum as lube, I slid all the way down again.

I couldn't believe I was jacking off to the woman who'd milked every drop of my cum from my body with her cunt and ass only a few days before.

She moaned, and her breaths grew shallow. Her fingers plunged into her heat, first one, then two, followed by three. I pumped my own cock to her rhythm.

She writhed and gasped, biting her lips.

God, I loved the way she looked when she was about to go over. Just as the narrator ordered "come for me," Henna tossed her head back, crying out her release. My dick followed, making me clench my teeth as my semen spewed from the head and covered my fist in hot shots.

I watched Henna as she continued to come. She was so fucking beautiful. I could have almost sworn she gasped my name, but with the sounds of the book, I couldn't be sure.

As she calmed from her orgasmic high, her body slumped back, leaving a dreamy look on her face. Her sexy-as-sin breasts heaved, and the light tinge of sweat on her abdomen made me crave to lick her stomach and the slick folds of her cunt.

Her phone beeped, breaking the spell.

Henna sighed, reaching over to retrieve her mobile from the side table. She turned off the audiobook and read the display.

"I guess there's no rest for the wicked," she muttered to herself, slipping her legs over the side of the hammock and heading inside her room.

I looked down at my cum-covered hand and still-hard cock.

This was fucking great.

The woman was Viagra to my libido. After I figured out a way to get her to forgive me, I planned to fuck her until she couldn't walk and every man on the island knew she was mine from the number of times she cried out my name as she came.

CHAPTER FIFTEEN

Zack

"MR. LYKAIOS, please stand over there. We want to make sure there are no shadows on your face when the photographer begins." A small, portly older man with a receding hairline and clothes meant for a man smaller than him pointed to a spot next to Henna.

I nodded my agreement and took my position. Henna glanced over her shoulder, not saying a word, and then looked out toward the deep aqua water of the Pacific.

She hadn't gotten over her irritation with me. No matter how many times I tried to speak with her in private, she ignored me or found every opportunity to avoid me.

"You're going to have to talk to me sometime."

"No, I'm not." She smiled as a reporter asked her to

pose, then relaxed. "You invaded a project that was in motion for a stupid photo op. If you wanted pictures for your social media, I could have snapped a few shots with my cellphone and called it a day. Now because of this—" she gestured to everyone around us, "—actual work won't start for at least a few more days, which means we are now behind schedule on what was already a tight deadline."

I winced. She was right about the spectacle. Photographers and media outlets from all the major travel and business sites and journals had sent representatives to the now-dubbed "groundbreaking event."

Nearly every hotel in the vicinity was booked to capacity, and I had a full day of interviews ahead.

"I'm sorry."

"If you're truly sorry, you'll handle all the interviews today while Charlie and I work."

"That was the plan."

Her rigid demeanor changed, and she turned. "Are you serious?"

"Yes."

Relief flashed in her gaze, making me realize how stressed she was about the project. "Thank you."

"You're very welcome. I'm sure I can find a way for you to make it up to me."

She pursed her lips and shook her head. "Of course, you can. Too bad it's not going to happen again."

I stroked a finger down the back of one of her arms.

"You say that every time. I don't think it means what you think it means."

Her features completely transformed from all-business to pure delight, and my heart clenched tight.

Had she ever looked at me with such pure joy before? I'd seen her in the throes of passion and more than my share of anger, but this made me crave to put that expression on her face every day for the rest of my life.

Fuck, where the hell had that come from?

"You quoted my favorite movie."

"*The Princess Bride.* It's a classic. Every man should have it in his arsenal to disarm prickly card sharks and corporate executives."

"Is that right?" Her eyes twinkled.

Just as I reached out to touch her face, Charlie nudged my shoulder.

"Let's get this waste of time over with and flirt later." Her refined accent was unable to hide her annoyance.

"Always a pleasure seeing you, Charlie. How are your parents? No luck in shackling you to some duke or prince yet?"

Charlie came from the upper echelon of Norway. Her mother was Norwegian nobility and her father was the head of one of the largest oil companies in Northern Europe. Charlotte "Charlie" Skaugum was supposed to be married and producing the next generation of stodgy aristocrats. Instead, Charlie had changed her last name to Steel and chose to go a different route, which scandalized her family.

I'd known Charlie since her first project, which had also happened to be HPZ's first project. We'd hired her on recommendation from a friend and never regretted it. Well, except when she would bite our heads off for interfering in her plans.

This was probably the reason she and Henna got along so well. They hated anything that interrupted their schedules.

We'd maintained a friendship over the years since and teamed up on various projects. Charlie would give me tips on possible spots for resorts and I would send her clients who wouldn't annoy her with their neediness.

"Shut it, Lykaios. Or next time I'll stab you with one of my X-Acto knives for messing up my day. You're only alive today because Henna talked me down from my vengeance."

"Well I guess I'll have to thank her." I paused. "Later. In private."

Both Henna and Charlie rolled their eyes.

"And there we have it. Inside every twenty-something bazillionaire is a prepubescent teen ready to jump out." Charlie glared at Henna. "I really can't believe you're sleeping with him. I thought you had better taste."

"Who says anything is going on between us?" Henna challenged.

"Me. You two are human balls of pheromones."

I saw Henna's cheeks tinge with a faint blush. "I think we should get this thing started so people don't feel the need to talk too much."

Immediately the all-business mask was firmly back in place.

Charlie sighed. "You're the boss."

I WALKED INTO MY BUNGALOW, throwing my jacket on a nearby chair, and opened the top two buttons of my shirt. After pouring a glass of ice water the hotel staff had waiting on a tray by the entry table, I drank it down, letting the cold liquid cool my body.

I walked toward the back deck of the suite and stared out into the night. I wiped the light sheen of sweat from my brow.

The heat and humidity were too intense for a fucking suit, but it was what Henna said was necessary for the pictures, since the project photos were going to appear in business magazines all over the world and many wouldn't understand the casual nature of an island project.

It had taken me nearly six hours to get through all the

interviews I'd agreed to manage so Henna and Charlie could handle project logistics. My brain felt exhausted from answering the same damn questions for fifty different reporters.

Among them being many personal ones that annoyed the shit out of me.

Have you reconciled with your father?

What was the reason for the initial falling out?

Who was the mystery woman from the club?

Was your masked woman Ms. Henna Anthony? Is it casual, or something more?

I probably hadn't helped the speculation about my relationship with Henna when my attention would shift the second she came into view. She'd walked around the property talking with project staff, giving directions like a general. The way she handled everyone around her was like a hypnotizing dance.

I thought she hadn't noticed me suffering through interview after interview but then she'd walked over to the section I'd sat in for hours and offered to take over so I could have a break. What had surprised me was that she'd arranged for a private meal in a hotel office, away from any press or staff. It was a gesture that meant more to me than she knew.

When I'd returned, I found her holding court with various reporters, steering questions in the directions she wanted and playing the always efficient and knowledgeable Lykaios International's chief operations officer. She handled everyone in the same way she'd handled Dwight. She didn't outright flirt but made each and every person around her feel as if she was intently listening to them.

Then when she'd lifted her gaze from the reporters and saw me, there was a shift in her eyes, and I felt as if something had gripped my heart and squeezed.

I knew without a doubt I couldn't leave this island without setting things right with Henna. Hell, I couldn't leave without making it damn clear where we stood.

God, I was like a lovesick puppy unable to figure out which way was up. How the fuck had I gotten here? I wasn't a relationship guy, and all I could think about was keeping Henna. No matter what she said, she was a relationship woman.

Now I had to convince her I was the guy to take a chance on.

Taking a deep breath, I walked back into the bungalow and through my front door and moved toward Henna's. I set my hand on the wood of her door.

I knew she was inside. During dinner, Charlie had mentioned Henna was going to call it a night and have her meal in her room.

She was so much like me, needing time to completely turn off after long hours surrounded by people.

How would she react if I knocked? Would she let me in? Would she tell me to leave?

Man up, Lykaios. Stop being such a pussy and take a chance.

"Here goes."

I pushed the doorbell, feeling my heart in my throat.

CHAPTER SIXTEEN

Henna

MY HANDS SHOOK as I touched the wooden door. I hadn't needed to look through the peephole to know it was Zack.

If I opened it, everything would change. This thing between us would go from secret hookups to the public. To a relationship.

I shook my head.

Who was I kidding?

This was a relationship from that first night in his penthouse. Probably before that. But what kind?

The doorbell rang again, followed by a knock.

Lifting my fingers from the wood, I gripped the door handle and pulled.

My breath caught at the intensity of Zack's piercing blue gaze.

He wore the same clothes from earlier in the evening sans the jacket. His collar was open, hinting at the tattoos running along the left side of his body.

My core clenched, knowing what I was about to do.

"Tell me you want this." Zack took a step toward me. "Tell me this is more than a fast fuck whenever we're alone." He took another step, setting a hand on the doorframe and leaning forward until our foreheads touched. "Tell me you're going as insane by what you're feeling as I am."

I licked my lips and closed my eyes for a brief second before I said, "It's not just you."

He gripped my waist, walking me backward as he shut my door behind him.

"I need you to be sure." He cupped my face, tilting it so I stared up at him. "If we take this step, you're mine, Henna. No hiding that we're together, no flirting with other men, no private dinners with billionaires, and definitely no one in your bed but me."

"Do the rules apply to you as well?"

"Yes."

"What about your brothers? What about Collin? This thing between us could cause problems for both of us."

"As crazy as it is, what we have is a relationship. We

are a couple. I don't give a shit what anyone thinks about it but you."

The vehemence in his words and his gaze sent goosebumps over my skin.

I wanted to throw caution to the wind, but I had to be sure he understood the consequences of being involved with me.

"You say that now, but when we're back in Vegas it will change. Remember, many of your business associates dislike anyone or anything to do with the Anthony name."

"You're not your father. And I won't change my mind." Threading his fingers into my hair, he tilted my head back while rubbing his stubble along my neck. "Say yes, Henna, and see how intense and hot we burn together. You're the only woman to make me want this."

My fingers dug into his forearms as I arched into the rough abrasions of Zack's beard.

My heart pounded and my cleft grew slick.

"Yes. I want this."

"Thank God." Zack covered my lips with his.

His tongue pushed into my mouth, filling my taste buds with the flavor of whiskey and his unique essence.

I gripped the back of his head.

His kisses were like a drug, intoxicating and addictive. This need for him had grown so much more intense, so much more all-consuming since that first kiss following a girls' night at one of Hagen's clubs.

Lifting me against the hard ridge of his cock, Zack carried me toward the bedroom but then changed his mind and went out the back of the bungalow into the South Pacific breeze.

He laid me on the hammock positioned in the corner of the deck with my legs dangling off.

I lifted a brow.

Zack gave me a sheepish grin. "You have no idea how many times I've fantasized about fucking you here since I arrived yesterday. That red bikini of yours should be illegal."

"So, you were watching me?"

He leaned down, biting my lower lip and giving it a sting. "Yes, baby, I was watching, and I saw everything."

Heat and desire crept up my skin. "I know. I heard you from the other side of the partition. It served you right for messing up my dinner with Jai."

"How was I to know that he was your cousin? He could be just another rich bastard who wants in your pants like everyone else who encounters you."

"No matter what you seem to believe, not every man wants me."

"We'll agree to disagree."

"When did you become so possessive?"

"I'm not normally. It is you who brings out this side of me."

"Oh."

"Yes. Oh." He kissed me again as he worked the hem of my dress upward, over my hips and breasts. "Raise your arms, so I can take this off. I want nothing between me and your gorgeous skin."

I lifted my hands, following Zack's directions, and let him tug my dress over my head and throw it on the floor. Next, he gripped the sides of my thong, snapping the fabric.

He hummed in appreciation as he surveyed me from head to toe and then cupped my naked breasts with his large hands. "You are my fantasy come to life."

Leaning down, he took a nipple into his mouth, biting the tip and then sucking the sting away. I moaned and arched toward him.

"More," I gasped, clenching my fingers against the ropes of the hammock.

Zack smiled in response and moved to the other breast. His tongue circled, flicked, and teased before he nipped my sensitive bud with his teeth.

Until this man, I never enjoyed my pleasure mixed with the bite of pain. Now I craved more. What exactly, I wasn't sure.

All of a sudden, he pulled back and stood, leaving me panting and a bit confused.

"I'll be right back."

"What?"

"Relax. I promise I'll be only gone a few minutes."

I sighed. "Remember, you have a woman waiting to be serviced."

He gave me a breathtakingly wicked grin. "That is one thing I definitely won't forget."

Zack moved around the partition separating our two adjacent bungalows. The lock clicked on his sliding door as he opened it.

I stared up at the wooden beams of the roof above me, trying to relax until Zack returned.

What could be so important that he had to stop the fun?

The warm breeze picked up, sending goosebumps over my exposed skin. The hammock swayed, and I lifted my head to wonder where Zack was.

"I knew you wouldn't be able to wait long."

I frowned. "I'm naked and out in the open. I feel it isn't fair."

"Let's remedy that."

He set three lit candles on the outdoor dining table and began to strip. Instead of watching the sexy-as-sin man take off his clothes, I studied the candles. Red, green, blue.

"Are you planning to do what I think you're about to do?"

"Would you stop me if I was?"

I turned my attention to him and nearly swallowed my

tongue. He was shrugging out of his shirt, and the way his muscles flexed and released with each movement made me want to lick every inch of him.

His fingers went to the buttons of his pants and I hummed.

"Like what you see?"

"Absolutely. I want to see more."

How had we gone from intense to playful? Was this normal?

"Stop thinking." He stepped out of his pants, coming toward me and pulling me up.

He grazed his lips over mine. "This is us, Henna."

"You still have on your boxers."

"The second they come off, I'll want to be inside you, and I have plans for this gorgeous body."

"We can't have that."

He cupped my ass, pulling my pussy against his thick cock. I rubbed my cleft along his length, feeling my clit swell and core flood with need.

One of his hands crept into my hair, fisting the tangled mass before he kissed me again.

I sank into the intoxicating taste of him, stroking my tongue along his in a dueling dance of seduction. What was it about this man that took all rational thought from my head? I wanted to crawl into him and consume him.

Maybe it was knowing he wanted this to be real,

wanted to make this thing between us a relationship. I never thought there was love in my future, but right now with Zack I felt it would finally happen.

He broke the kiss and pushed me flat to the ropes of the hammock.

"Slide your body all the way up, spread-eagle, and grab the sides. Now hold still and don't let go. Enjoy this, Henna. The discomfort is worth the pleasure."

He picked up a candle, poured a small bit on his wrist and nodded. "Perfect temperature."

"I've never done this," I said, panting.

"But you want to."

"Yes." There was always pleasure in Zack's arms.

"Remember what I said. Hold still."

In the next second, I cried out as white-hot pain seized my stomach.

"Easy," Zack crooned while blowing on the blue wax pooling in my belly button.

The discomfort dulled and was released by a sensation I wasn't sure was real. It was cool and warm at the same time.

That was when I smelled it. "Eucalyptus."

"I've found it does well to ease the sting."

The thought of him with other women made me want to hit something. Logic said I had no reason to be jealous, but my emotions were all over the place.

"Hey." Zack turned my face toward his. "We're here. I'm with you, and you're with me."

Before I could respond, another splash of wax hit my skin, but this time it was green and in the valley of my breasts.

"Fuck." I arched up. "Zack."

A second later, the pain morphed into pleasure, one that I wanted to feel more and more of.

"I...I want."

He poured again and again.

"Oh God." I squeezed my eyes closed and reveled in the sensation. My pussy contracted, and my desire coated my thighs.

"Let go, baby. Get lost in the feeling." Zack pushed two fingers into me while he tilted the red candle.

"It's too much. Zack. Yes. Don't stop."

"I don't intend to." He pumped harder and then all of a sudden stopped. "You're so wet. Practically soaking my hand. I have to taste you. Don't move."

Zack dropped to his knees, pulling one leg wide and over his shoulder before his mouth landed on my pussy.

He ate at me like a man starved. My core trembled and then spasmed. I clenched down, detonating into ecstasy. I thrashed and moaned and begged. Why I begged I hadn't a clue.

"You taste better and better," he murmured as he

flicked his wicked tongue in and out of my trembling pussy.

He brought me over twice more before he rose, setting a knee on the ropes of the hammock.

I stared down my body to his gloriously naked one. His hard, thick cock jutted straight out and a dewy drop of precum beaded the top. Reaching down, I gathered his essence on my fingertip and then brought it to my lips.

"Mmmm," I hummed. "You taste pretty good yourself."

I pushed him onto his back, letting the hammock rock back and forth. Bits of wax fell over his chest as it flaked off mine with my movements. I paused, and for a split second I had a vision of what it would look like to see him covered in a bold color.

He watched me with a deep intensity as he rubbed his thick bare cock between the folds of my slick sex.

"If I wanted to, would you let me turn you into a canvas?"

He fisted my hair, drawing me down to his lips. "As long as you remember you belong to me, I'll let you do anything that gives you pleasure."

I smiled against his mouth, reached down, and positioned him at my soaked entrance.

"Henna." He held me up, refusing to let me sink down. "Condom."

I shook my head. "No condom. I want to feel you, every inch of you."

"But what if you get pregnant?"

"I'm on the pill and clean."

"I'm clean too." He gasped, not releasing his hold on my hips.

I teased the head of his cock with my pussy, shifting side to side.

"Then what are you waiting for?"

"Nothing." He plunged me down over his throbbing cock.

Stars flashed before my eyes as my slick tissues stretched to accommodate his hard length. I was on fire. I rose onto my knees and slid down, repeating the motion over and over. Zack's corded stomach punched and flexed as he resisted the urge to take control. The hammock rocked with my movements, giving me deeper and deeper penetrations.

His piercing blue eyes held my gaze, conveying desire and a need for me I'd never experienced with any other man.

"Henna. I'm not going to last."

I set my hand over his pecs. "Then let go. I'll catch you."

"Not without you."

He grabbed my thighs and thrust upward as I went down. I began to ride, hard and fast. The only sounds I could hear were the wet, dirty, pleasure-filled moans of our lovemaking.

I was completely lost as my release snuck up on me, and shortly after Zack followed, holding me down over his cock as he filled me with his cum.

CHAPTER SEVENTEEN

Zack

"*OJIISAN* IS IN THE LOUNGE. Follow me," Sota said in his usual no-nonsense way and directed me toward the private rooms of the club.

I nodded and made my way to the back of one of Draco's strip clubs.

It had been two weeks since I'd returned to Vegas, and my emotions were all over the place. It wasn't supposed to feel so right to be with her. It wasn't supposed to make me wish for more. And it definitely wasn't supposed to make me claim her as mine.

Every time we made love, it was more intense than the time before. Shit, had I just called it love?

It was a lot more than fucking. We could read each

other in ways I'd never experienced with anyone. It was as
if she crawled inside my body and made me feel and want
something more than taking down Collin.

I ran a hand through my hair.

Since Bora Bora, we'd slept in the same bed nearly
every night. It was as if neither of us could get any sleep if
the other wasn't near. We even talked. I couldn't remember
a time I wanted to share anything with a woman. She made
me feel like there was really someone out there for me.

No matter what I'd believed in the past, I couldn't hurt
her. I wouldn't hurt her with my plan. She meant too damn
much to me, and I couldn't lose her.

Now I could only hope Draco would agree to the
change.

It was as if the bastard knew I wanted to cancel. He'd
made me wait two weeks for an appointment. And it
wasn't as if I could walk into his club and demand a
meeting. No matter how much we got along, he was still a
mob boss and followed the rules of respect ingrained in
him from his youth as a member of the Yakuza.

I passed booths for private dances and through the
social area of the club. It always surprised me how Draco
managed to make all his strip clubs look classy and high
end. Everyone who entered any of his establishments knew
his "girls" were treated with respect and any breaking of
the rules could result in dire consequences.

Two of Draco's personal guards stood outside of the

drape-covered entrance to the private club offices. I
nodded to them and without responding, they lifted the
curtains, stepping aside.

*"My grandsons tell me you requested a meeting. You
will excuse the delay. I was on holiday."* Draco spoke in
Japanese while taking a sip of the green tea he preferred
over spirits.

Draco held court with various men situated around
him. Some with scantily clad women serving them drinks
and others with dancers giving them personal lap dances.

"Oyabun, could we speak in private?" I responded in
his native tongue.

During the years Hagen worked for Draco, Hagen
made it mandatory for Pierce and me to learn Japanese.
Draco, as far as we knew, had been our benefactor and
deserved for us to show him respect by speaking to him in
Japanese when appropriate.

Draco lifted his hand and cleared his throat.
Immediately, everyone grew quiet and stopped whatever
they were doing.

"Out," Draco ordered.

It took less than a minute for the rooms to clear out
with the exception of Draco's security and grandsons. All
eleven of them were in house today, and it seemed like they
were very interested in the discussion about to happen as
they took seats near their grandfather.

Draco gestured to the now-empty sofa next to him. I

took my seat and waited for the nod to say it was time to start.

This was one part of meeting with Draco that drove me crazy. The old man would make me wait longer than anyone else to drill into my head that I had no patience.

After a solid five minutes, he said, *"Talk."*

"I want the plan to stop. There are too many consequences if it goes through."

"The consequences aren't greater than any other time before. Does this have to do with Anthony's daughter?"

I hesitated, not wanting Henna's name spoken by the man who'd destroyed her life. But I had to tell him the truth.

"Yes. I won't hurt her."

"So she's worth stopping the plan after all these years?"

"Yes. She's worth more to me than anything else."

Draco picked up his teacup, took a sip, set the drink down, and then leaned back in his leather seat. *"This is nearly ten years of planning and execution. I'm not sure I want to stop course."*

My temper rose. *"You owe it to her for what you did to her. You owe it to me for creating the lie that became my life."*

Surprise flashed on Draco's face. *"So you know? I wondered if Hagen would tell you."*

"Why would you do this to us? We were children. Why

would you do it to two little girls and a widow, who had already suffered so much?"

"Because it is what I do. It is what was expected of me. My family has rules. One doesn't slight them, and most of all, one doesn't steal from them. That is what Anthony did. He took the coward's way out and so his heirs had to pay the price."

"How could you believe taking a child from their family was just payment for the sins of their father?"

"It is the way it was meant to be. It was better than following the tradition of my childhood. Then there would be no Anthonys left in the world."

I bit the inside of my cheek to keep my temper from erupting.

When Hagen had told me Draco had planned to take either Henna or Anaya as a "companion" for his granddaughter to make restitution for Victor Anthony's crimes, I'd felt my stomach roll and an anger I'd never experienced fill my body. Learning the truth had opened my eyes to the type of man I'd idolized for the last ten years.

There was no sugarcoating who Draco was—he was a ruthless mobster.

"And Collin? He never did anything against your family."

"He stood between me and my revenge. So I took what was most precious to him."

A lump formed in my throat. *"His sons."*

"Yes." There was a tinge of regret in that one word I hadn't expected to hear.

Up until this point, there was no apology for the past, but now I wasn't sure. He was right—he'd behaved as any mob boss was expected to behave. Any sign of weakness and his competitors would think his territory was up for grabs. It didn't excuse him. I lost my childhood, my time with my mother, my time with my father. Hell, I'd lost my sister.

"Cancel the buyout and we'll call it even."

"That is all it will take to make it business as usual?"

I wanted to say *hell no*, but Draco was a part of our world, and there was no truly getting out of working for him.

Just as Henna was never going to be free of Eric Donavon. She could view it as a friendship, but she was tied to a man heavily connected to the European underworld.

We were definitely going to have to figure things out on that account.

"Yes."

"I never thought I'd see the day." Draco laughed. *"You love something more than your need to best Collin."*

God, was I in love with her?

Yes. She was my match in everything. And she saw something in me that was worthy.

"*So we have a deal?*"

Draco studied me and after a few seconds, smiled, and said, "*Yes.*"

I almost sagged in relief.

"*However, I want something in return for my efforts.*"

"*And what would you like?*"

"*A meeting with Hagen. The boy sends others for things I expect him to complete.*"

"*I'll see what I can do.*"

"*The boy is stubborn.*"

"*It's a family trait.*"

"*Yes. I heard your baby sister is very much like you.*"

"*Anaya is not part of any negotiations.*"

"*Calm yourself. It was an observation.*"

"*I will take my leave.*"

Draco nodded, and I rose from my seat.

As I stepped toward the exit, Draco said, "*Friendly warning: the Anthony women are part of worlds you should keep your eyes on. Especially that baby sister of yours.*"

I almost turned to question him but thought better of it and headed out the door.

CHAPTER EIGHTEEN

Henna

"I'LL PICK you up at five. It will give us two hours to drive to your house, change, and return to Vegas for the Firewater party at Ida," Zack instructed as I answered my office phone.

He'd called just as I escaped to my office for a quick break between meetings. Today's schedule was packed with new project discussions and meetings. Meetings where I felt as if I were talking to a group of preschoolers with the way the board members argued.

When Collin had decided to take in outside investors, I'd advised against it. But he'd insisted we needed new blood to give us a bigger vision. Now both of us had to deal with high-maintenance board members and investors who wanted to argue about everything from the type of towels used at resorts to the sod planted at golf courses. If I were them, I'd worry about wasting time and money with menial discussions.

It also burned me that they viewed me as an underling, when in fact I could buy each of those assholes out without thinking twice.

"You do realize it's only noon? I have to get through the remainder of the board meeting before I can even consider celebrating Penny's newest line of whiskey."

"She's your cousin. I was given strict instructions to get you to the party on time."

"The way it's looking, I may strangle someone before the day is out."

"Want me to come rescue you?"

"Sure, that's going to help. Remember, you're public enemy number one."

After Bora Bora, the media had caught wind of my relationship with Zack and had latched on. They wanted all the details, especially since we'd been rivals for years. This also caused a lot of issues with the board members, many of them saying our relationship was a conflict of interest and I was putting the company at risk for a hostile takeover with my romance.

Over the last few weeks, Zack and I had come to an understanding. Business was business and that was separate from what we had.

And what we had was intense and easy at the same time. We got each other, much to our families' great surprise. No one could wrap their heads around the fact Zack was in a committed relationship or the fact I was the woman he was with. Even Collin, who initially was worried Zack was using me, had come around. Though nothing had changed on the front of him and Zack.

Now here I was, months in and with no regrets.

"As long as you know I'm not the enemy, I don't give two shits what those old bastards think." There was a fierceness to his words that made me realize he still worried about how I saw him.

"Zack," I sighed. "You know how I feel about you. Do you think I would let any man move into my house if he wasn't important to me?"

"Then say it."

"Say what?" I knew what he wanted me to tell him.

We both felt it but were too afraid to speak the words. We knew saying them meant we were vulnerable to the other.

"The words I want to hear."

"You say it first."

"Damn stubborn woman. You know exactly what you mean to me."

"You've never told me."

"I tell you every time I make love to you, every time you fall asleep in my arms. Hell, I tell you every time a damn reporter sticks his microphone in my face asking about us and I don't punch him because you don't want that kind of publicity for our relationship."

I smiled at the last part of his statement. Zack had literally refrained from killing a journalist who dared to ask him about my father a few weeks ago. His protectiveness over me was beyond anything I could imagine.

"Wouldn't it be better to say it when we're face to face?"

"You can say it then too."

"Fine." I waited, staring out my window toward the Nevada desert.

"Please, baby." There was a plea in his voice that had me caving. "Let me hear you say it."

"I love you, Zack."

He released a deep breath as if he'd been holding it. "God, I've wanted to hear that for months."

"Now you say it."

"So demanding." He chuckled. "I lov—"

He stopped mid-word as I heard a bunch of commotion in the background and then a bunch of muffled voices. Then I heard, "Fuck, this cannot be happening."

"Zack," I called. "Zack, dammit, answer me. What's wrong?"

"Henna." There was a sense of anguish in his voice. "I promise, I'll fix this. I promise. Just know I love you, baby."

"Zack, you aren't making any sense."

"I'm on my way. I need you to believe me when I say it wasn't supposed to go through."

He hung up.

What the hell just happened?

Before I could call Zack back and demand he tell me what was going on, Collin walked in.

His face was ashen and etched with shock.

I ran to him. "What is it?"

I pulled him toward my desk chair, making him sit.

"He actually did what he said he would. He actually took my company from me. He got his revenge."

"What? Who?" I couldn't grasp what he was talking about. Then it hit me.

"No, he wouldn't. He wouldn't do that to me. He..."

Collin handed me a set of papers. "This came via courier. It was timed to arrive during the break. It's signed."

As I read the document, I couldn't believe what I was seeing. It was a note from Draco.

This ends any and all claims for past grievances.

DJ

I flipped to the next page and felt like my world was spinning. Half of all the partners on the board had sold their stock to ZL Holdings, giving control of the board to Zack. And then the financial conglomerate that financed all of Lykaios International's projects and held all its debt had been bought out by a shell corporation linked to Zack.

He essentially owned Lykaios International. Everything and anything the company did had to get Zack's approval.

I felt dizzy, and my stomach churned. This explained why so many of the board had insisted on an earlier break than during usual sessions. They wanted to leave before the news got to us.

My hands shook. "I'm so sorry, Collin. This is my fault."

"No, it's mine."

"I let my guard down. I trusted him. I brought this on you."

God, I'd let him into my home, into my heart. I'd told him I loved him.

I was such a fool.

"I promise I will get your company back."

"Henna!" A shout came from outside my office, making me freeze and my anger rise.

CHAPTER NINETEEN

Zack

I RUSHED into Henna's office to find devastation across Collin's and Henna's faces as they looked up from the papers.

"What have you done?" Henna stomped toward me. "Is your need for revenge so much that you'd destroy everything a good man who has known nothing but pain built?"

"Let me explain..."

"I don't want to hear anything. You used me. Made me believe you were worth lowering my guard. I see what a mistake it was."

"Henna, it wasn't supposed to go through. I cancelled the buyout."

"Bullshit. Then how did these papers get filed with the board? How did the stock transfer over to you? How did your company become the holder of all our financial debt?"

"Who sent those to you?"

"Your pal Draco sent them with a flower basket."

I had no idea how to explain any of it. When the courier brought over the delivery, I had no idea what was inside. The only things on my mind were reveling in hearing Henna tell me she loved me and trying to figure out how to get her to agree to spend the rest of her life with me.

Now everything was shot to hell.

No matter what I said, there was no way for me to defend myself. And the look in her eyes told me she wouldn't believe me even if I tried.

"Fuck." I gripped my hair, feeling everything I'd built with Henna over the past few months shatter into a million pieces.

Why would Draco do this after I'd made it clear my plans had changed? Hell, he was the person to truly make me realize what I felt for Henna was love.

"You think you were clever, going after all the various partners to buy them out. Well, you've met your match. I will stop at nothing until I take everything from you as you have Collin."

"Henna, *paidi mou*. It's okay."

"No, Collin, it isn't. Even after everything, he can't

forgive." She poked a finger in my chest. "Know this, Zacharias Lykaios. You think Draco is a scary motherfucker? The people I know will make him look like a sweet old grandpa. Hell hath no fury like a woman scorned and all that jazz."

I looked at Collin. "I'll sign it back to you. I don't want it."

"Get out and don't come back. Your days of using me are over." Henna's voice quivered for a brief second before she clenched her jaw.

"Please, Henna. Baby, listen to me."

"Don't ever call me that again." Her eyes were so cold, like nothing I'd seen before. "From this moment on, we are enemies as I'd always believed and foolishly forgotten."

Collin approached Henna, setting a hand on her waist, and her shoulders immediately slumped. It killed me to know I was the one to hurt her.

I tried to reach out to touch Henna, but Collin lifted his hand, stopping me, and said, "Son, I believe it's a good idea for you to leave. We will talk soon."

Even after all this, he still called me son, but the command in his tone reminded me of when I was a child and I'd done something to upset Mama with my antics.

I nodded, dropping my hand, and walked toward the door. As I stepped over the threshold, I said, not looking behind me, "For what it's worth, I wasn't pretending, Henna. It was all real. I fell in love with you."

I walked out, in a daze.

Half an hour later, I found myself at the Ida taking the private elevator to Hagen and Penny's penthouse.

The cab doors had barely opened before Hagen grabbed me and punched me, knocking me to the ground. Stars exploded behind my eyes.

Fuck. No wonder Draco had used Hagen as an enforcer. One of his punches would make the strongest men cry.

Hagen hurled me up with my shirt and towered over me. "You stupid asshole. How the fuck could you do this? Did you for one goddamned minute think about us? Obviously not. You seem to only think about yourself and your damn need to get revenge."

I said nothing, which resulted in another fist to the face. I deserved it. There was no point in defending myself.

Penny ran in. "Hagen, put him down. This isn't how to handle it."

"I think it's the perfect way to handle it." Pierce came around the hallway corner of the penthouse leading out of the living-room area. "Punch him again."

"Don't you dare, Hagen Lykaios." Penny stalked over. "It's not going to change anything."

"Let him kick my ass. It can't make me feel any worse than I already do." I felt blood drip down the side of my jaw.

"Shut up, Zack. You've caused enough trouble for three lifetimes." Amelia walked up to me with her arms crossed. "I'm really happy I left Christopher with my parents today. The last thing I need him to see are his uncles acting like rejects from an MMA clown competition."

Hagen stopped glowering at me to send a death stare to Amelia, who wasn't fazed in the least.

When his attention returned to me, I braced for another blow, but it never came. Instead, Hagen threw me to the floor and walked away.

"Fight back, dammit." Pierce egged me on.

"No." I pushed myself to sitting, wiped my bloody mouth on my sleeve, and tried to keep the lights flashing behind my eyes at bay.

"Drink this." Hagen crouched down in front of me and handed me a glass with what I assumed was Firewater by its rose-tinged liquid.

The disappointment on his face was like a blow to the gut.

I took a deep swig of the potent alcohol. I was going to need the whole bottle to numb the pain.

"It wasn't supposed to happen the way it did."

"What way was it supposed to happen?" Pierce asked, taking a seat on the floor next to me. "You never hid your desire for revenge, but I never thought you'd go behind our backs to accomplish it."

I winced.

"When I set the plan in motion, we all hated him."

"And after you found out the truth about the past and Anaya?" Pierce grabbed my glass and swallowed the remainder of my drink.

"I lost sight of the plan. When I realized it was in motion, I cancelled the shares buyout. But Draco still went through with the deal." I dropped my head to my knees. "I don't expect any of you to believe me."

"From the way we see it, if knowing the truth about Anaya and the past wouldn't change your mind, nothing would." Hagen sat in front of me, handing me the bottle of Firewater. "Why would you give up your plan when it was in your grasp?"

"Because he's in love with Henna." Collin's voice came from the archway leading into the penthouse. "You broke her heart, boy. More than that idiot Hunter ever did. I want to know what you're going to do to fix it."

I stared at the man who'd been my enemy since I was eighteen and he'd thrown me out of our home. There was only love and sadness in his eyes. How had I never noticed it before?

"Do you truly hate me so much, son?"

I pushed up to my feet, trying to ignore the throbbing in my head.

I made my way to where Collin stood.

When I was a foot away from him, I said, "No. I

wanted to. I tried, and maybe not being able to was the reason I was so determined."

"It killed me to hurt you." Tears filled Collin's eyes. "But I had to protect your sister—she was a mere babe."

"I know," I whispered and then dropped my head. "I'm sorry. I'm so sorry."

"I'm the one who's sorry." Collin pulled me toward him, wrapping his arms around me.

For the first time since I was a small child, I felt the comfort of the father I'd adored. The father who'd made everything better even when I'd caused more trouble than I should.

He felt so small and frail now.

"Papa." I gripped Collin tight and began to cry.

Henna

"ANA, for the last time. I'll be back. I just need to figure things out," I said for the tenth time since I'd gotten on the phone with Anaya.

I'd spent the last day in transit from Vegas. I'd landed in Athens and then immediately boarded a helicopter to take me to my final destination. I'd called Collin last night but couldn't reach him and then again this morning but only got his voicemail.

I couldn't blame him for unplugging. I'd have done the same thing. Hell, the explosion of yesterday was the reason I was on this copter in the first place.

Before I'd left, I'd made a stop by the office and left a formal resignation letter. There was no way I could work for Lykaios International without Collin at the helm. Or with the knowledge I hadn't protected Collin from our enemies.

"Well, how would you feel if you showed up to my house and it was missing all your clothes and no note saying you were leaving town, much less the country? Hell, I spoke to you yesterday morning and you were talking about taking a spa vacation in Colorado. I know you aren't in Colorado."

"I needed a break. You're the one who's always telling me that I need to take a vacation. That's what I'm doing."

"For the love of God, at least tell me where you're going. I can find out if you push me to it. I'm resourceful."

"Where do I go whenever I need to recharge?"

"*Yia Yia* Sylvia's," she guessed. "I hope you called and aren't just showing up. You know how annoyed she gets when any of us pop in and she hasn't had a chance to cook."

"Yes, she knows. I'm not crazy enough to fly near her

island without letting her know. She's likely to have one of her men shoot the helicopter down."

"Point taken. Do you want me to fly over? I'm sure I can sweet-talk Collin into letting me..." Anaya trailed off. "Well, fuck. Does all the news mean Zack owns everything? Like in hostile takeover?"

I closed my eyes, trying to hold in the pain.

I will not cry. I will not cry.

"Exactly that."

"So that means you aren't on vacation. You quit your job."

I released a sigh. "Don't tell Mummy. At least until I get back and can fly to Arizona to tell her in person."

"You mean like how you told me I'm your half sister?"

"That's not fair. You know I wanted to tell you."

"I know. I'm just bitchy that I came back to Vegas and have to live in a mega mansion all alone."

"Well, you can go back to campus housing if that's more your jam."

"I'm young but not a moron. I'll stay in the multimillion-dollar palace you call a house with around-the-clock security and an on-call chef who will deliver prepared meals for whatever diet I want to try on a whim."

"Then what are you bitching at me about?"

"I'm worried about you. No one had to tell me to know you're in love with—"

"Don't say his name again. I know he's your brother,

but God." I pressed my fingers to the bridge of my nose and tried to control the tremor in my voice. "Don't I ever learn?"

"You're my sister and my loyalty will forever be to you. There is no question that I will punch him for what he did to you and Collin."

I smiled. "I love you, Ana."

"Back at you. Tell *Yia Yia* I said hi."

"I will. We're about to land."

"Call me if you need anything. I only have one class on campus and all the others are online so call me if you need to talk."

"I promise."

We hung up as the helicopter landed. I took a deep breath and straightened my appearance. I didn't want Sylvia to see I'd spent most of my flight over crying. I had to keep it together.

Then, after a few days, I was going to broach the subject with Sylvia and Eric about doing to Zack what he'd done to Collin.

CHAPTER TWENTY

Henna

"HEY, I was listening to my book," I exclaimed when Sylvia jerked my legs as I lounged in a deck chair on one of the many terraces overlooking the sea surrounding her private island.

The day was beautiful, with bright blue skies, a calm ocean, and a light breeze to keep the heat from becoming overwhelming. Perfect weather to get some sun.

I expected Sylvia to pounce on me the moment I arrived on the island, but all she'd done was take a look at me, kiss my forehead, and tell me to go eat and relax.

And that was what I'd done for the last week. She hadn't probed or asked me any questions about the takeover news that had hit all the business and travel journals. She hadn't batted an eye when I'd left the island phone off the hook after Zack called for probably the hundredth time. Sylvia knew I needed to take a step away from everything and everyone.

Especially Zack.

Our relationship was a big topic for the gossip sites and my heart was bleeding out, knowing I loved a man who'd betrayed me. I wished so much I could turn it off.

All I could do was keep a brave face when around others and cry when I was alone.

I wasn't pretending, Henna. It was all real. I fell in love with you.

The words he'd said when he left my office haunted me and made me hurt more. How could he love me and do what he'd done?

I wanted him to feel the same pain I felt. I knew as soon as I left the island, I'd begin my plans. Collin would get everything he'd lost back.

"I've called your name three times. I was getting tired waiting for you to respond," Sylvia said to me in Greek as she tapped her foot and crossed her arms across her body.

"A simple touch could have had the same effect, not the bulldozer punch you gave me," I responded in Greek.

My mother thought it important I learn the language in addition to her native tongue and English. My father, at the time, was involved in a lot of business dealings in

Greece and it also helped in talking to my cousins, since my aunt had married into a Greek family.

"If you want a punch, I'm more than happy to demonstrate. Amelia taught me many things." Sylvia lifted a brow, giving me her stern look that would have scared the shit out of anyone who didn't know her.

Sylvia had to create a dangerous reputation to make it in the male-dominated shipping world. The things she'd done were no more than many of her counterparts engaged in, but the fact she was female made her tactics scandalous.

"I'm not frightened of you. I know you have a soft spot for me. After all, I'm your mini-me."

"Stubborn is what you are. Don't think I'm not aware you're stalling. Let's go. I've let you wallow in your self-pity, now it's time to talk. And no more of your dirty books."

"You're one to talk. I'm listening to the book you recommended."

"You are mistaken. I'm a respectable widowed retiree."

I sat up. *"Who likes dirty, sexy books as much as I do."*

"Stop stalling and get your ass up." Sylvia turned without seeing if I was behind her.

No getting out of this conversation. Standing, I slipped on my swimsuit coverup and followed Sylvia up the stairs to the second level of the mansion and into her private sitting room.

"Sit."

I sighed and followed her order, taking my customary

spot on the couch I'd occupied numerous times over the years. *"For a sweet old lady, you're sure bossy."*

Sylvia tucked a few stray strands of her gray-speckled-with-black hair behind her ear before she settled in her armchair. She watched me, reaching for her cup of tea. She took a sip and set the saucer back on the table in front of her without taking her gaze from me.

This was her customary process right before she laid into me about something or another.

"Henna, you will not do what I know you're planning. I forbid it."

I stared at her, not sure I heard her correctly. Was she really protecting Zack?

"You can't be on his side. He...he...destroyed a good man. A man—"

Sylvia cut me off, *"—who threw his children out on the street when they were barely grown."*

"It wasn't his fault. Draco forced his hand." I hated knowing what Collin had done to Hagen, Pierce, and Zack.

"It doesn't change what happened. He left scars on those boys."

"That doesn't excuse what Zack did. He knew the truth and still went through with his plan."

"Don't make me smack you. If you weren't so hard-headed, you would have heard that boy out. Zacharias cancelled the plan right after he returned from Bora Bora."

"Then how did it go through?"

"Henna, Zacharias was involved with Draco. Rarely, if ever, will a man like him—" she paused, *"—or a woman like me, change plans. There is just too much time, energy, and money involved."*

Sylvia was right. Getting involved with anyone with underground ties meant taking a risk.

"Would you have pushed the buyout through, even if I asked you not to?"

"I would if it meant all debts were paid in full. Isn't that what Draco said in the note to you? In the world you live on the edge of, there is a code, and one doesn't just write off a debt. There is always a price to pay. Collin understands it, even if you don't."

"But it was the legacy he was going to leave to his grandchildren. Zack took what Collin was planning to give him in the long run." I ran a hand over my face. *"He was so devastated. You should have seen him."*

Sylvia's face softened. *"No, sweetheart. The reason Collin was so upset was because it was the legacy he was going to leave to his daughter. You."*

Me?

Immediately, tears filled my eyes. Sylvia was right. I was Collin's daughter, and he was everything Victor Anthony wasn't to me. Collin taught me so much and loved me as any father would.

"I never expected this. I'd planned to convince him to

let me buy into the company as a way to protect Lykaios International. To ensure his legacy lived on. I never wanted the company for myself. He's given me so much already."

Sylvia reached over the table and took my hand in hers. "A parent's love is unconditional and doesn't require repayment. Ask your mother. She's spent the last two decades protecting you and your sister."

"But that doesn't change what Zack did."

"This plan was in motion for nearly ten years. Going to Draco was a big step for him. I spoke to him a few days ago. He confirmed all past grievances against Collin and your family are clear."

"You spoke to him and didn't tell me?"

"I'm telling you now."

"I don't understand what I am supposed to do with all this information. It doesn't change what happened. Collin still lost everything."

"And no matter the reasons, Collin hurt his sons. You tell me, will revenge against Zacharias make the hurt any easier? Will it make you stop loving him?"

"What am I supposed to do? I hurt so much inside. I let him in. I gave him more than I've ever given anyone else."

"If there is truly no hope, then you need to heal, forgive him, and then move on. The anger will make you bitter and a shell of the woman you are."

"How do I heal? How do I stop loving him?"

"Time heals. How to stop loving him, that's a harder

one. If it was the real thing, it may never stop. All you can do is live life and see if it leads you to someone else."

The thought of another man in my life was something I couldn't even consider at this moment. I'd given parts of myself to Zack that I'd never explored with any other man. A vision flashed in my mind of Zack with another woman and my stomach clenched in pain.

"I know what you're thinking. It will happen if you can't forgive him. That man has called multiple times a day since you arrived."

"I need time."

"You've had a week to wallow. I've already made the arrangements for you to get off the island for a few days. Then you have to go back to America and figure out your life."

"And where am I going?" I studied Sylvia.

She gave me a smile. "To Monte Carlo, of course. Eric has your usual townhouse rented. He promised to help take your mind off reality for a few days."

"Eric and I are friends. Don't try to play matchmaker."

Sylvia's eyes grew big and she shook her head. "No, no, no. That man is not for you. He needs someone from his world. A woman to challenge him but accept who he is."

"Then this is for fun?"

"Yes. I know how much you like to empty snobby European elitist pockets."

She was right. It was always a thrill to take money from

those who thought they were better because their family was related to some far-off royal and had money for centuries. Those people played cards not to lose, whereas I played using logic and the drive to win.

"In other words, you're evicting me?"

"Yes. Staying here and hiding is no longer an option."

CHAPTER TWENTY-ONE

Zack

"MR. LYKAIOS, WE HAVE ARRIVED."

"Thank you, Jean," I said to my driver as I stepped out in front of the address in Monte Carlo that Sylvia Thanos had sent me a little after ten in the evening. My stomach was in knots. I wasn't sure what I'd do if Henna refused to see me. I'd spent nearly every waking moment of the last two weeks trying to fix the mess I'd created, trying to make up for the pain I'd caused my family, trying to find a way to get Henna to forgive me.

Hagen and Pierce were still pissed to holy hell with me. They felt as if I'd gone behind their backs, and I knew I had. We had always been a team, taking action only after we'd discussed every aspect and consequence. Making the deal with Draco was a betrayal against everything we'd built. I knew eventually they'd come around.

What had surprised me was how easily Collin had forgiven me. After that night in Hagen's penthouse, it felt like I had the father I'd lost so long ago. I hadn't realized how much I needed Collin in my life, even if it was to work through the past.

Now I had to fix things with Henna. Or at least I hoped I could. It had killed me to pack up my things from her house. Anaya was going to be staying there and I wasn't sure what to say to her. She was my sister but Henna's too. I expected her loyalties to stay with Henna. When I'd gone into the house, Anaya had been waiting for me, ready to pounce.

She'd given me an earful about how I'd destroyed the best thing that could ever happen to me. Then, when she was done riding my ass, she'd thrown her arms around my neck and hugged me, telling me she was so happy to be able to hug her big brothers now that the truth was out. Holding her had me crying for the second time in twenty-four hours.

Thank God I got myself under control, or Hagen and Pierce would never let me hear the end of it if they got wind of it. At least I could say I was the first of us to have a conversation with our sister about all the secrets surrounding our childhood and mother. One day soon, we all would have to get together and hash everything out.

But first I had to get my woman back.

I walked up the steps to the three-story French villa and rang the doorbell. After a few moments, a man in a tailored suit opened the door.

He inspected me from head to toe. I was dressed similar to him in a black-and-white tuxedo. The same one I'd worn to the opening of Henna's show at the Cypress.

After he decided I looked appropriate, the butler said in French, *"Invitation, please."*

I handed him the envelope with the invitation to the private event I was attending. The butler spoke into a wrist mic, looked up at me again, nodded, and then gestured for me to enter the house with a wave of his hand.

As I moved into the building, I noticed the armed security positioned discreetly along the outside wall of the house and the inside foyer. Security for tonight was beyond what I expected. But then again, the people invited to the party were individually worth hundreds of millions, if not billions.

I followed a long hallway that opened into a giant room that I could only describe as what one would see inside a French chateau, with an opulent white-and-gold ceiling, giant crystal chandelier, and antique furniture and artwork. However, instead of being a warm, inviting home, it was a private casino. Roulette and craps tables lined the edge of the space, with poker tables strategically placed to allow for comfort. It was a similar setup to the high-roller rooms at my casinos, but with the extra effect of armed security walking the periphery of the room.

"So, you showed up." A man with almost white-blond hair and olive skin came up to me.

Eric Donavon was as good looking up close as he was from across a ballroom. But no matter how much I wanted to dislike him, his connections to the mob, and his relationship with Henna, I had to give the man credit for arranging this night and wanting to see Henna happy.

God, I hoped I could make her happy. She fucking deserved some happiness.

"Looks that way." I offered Donavon my hand. "Thank you for inviting me."

He took it and then said in a low whisper, "If you hurt her again, Sylvia isn't the only one you will have to worry about coming after you."

This wasn't the first time in the last two weeks I'd heard that line. Everyone from my brothers to Collin and Anaya had given me the same warning.

I knew I'd hurt Henna, and the fact she'd all but secluded herself on Sylvia's island showed the depth of her pain. Because of her past, she never ran away from hardship. But the fact she had done so screamed the depth of how much I'd fucked up.

I could only hope I hadn't destroyed any chance of her forgiving me.

"You'll have to get in line."

Donovan smiled. "Henna does bring out a passionate response from those who love her. We all want to protect the woman who makes the world believe she is stronger than all of us, but who is actually the most vulnerable."

"I suggest you never say that to her face."

Donovan pointed to the stairs. "She is upstairs in the room to the right. The buy-in is one million. Once you pay, the attendant will grant you access."

I nodded, turning toward the grand staircase. I glanced over my shoulder. "Thanks again."

"Thank me by losing a lot of money in my casino and making my girl smile again."

"I'll do my best."

I worked my way around waiters and party attendees before I reached the poker room. I glanced inside, finding Henna waiting with a group of players for the next game to start. There was an empty seat next to her that I knew was left open just for me. I'd have to remember to send Eric a bottle of Firewater as a thanks.

I approached the banker, handed her double the buy-in amount, and collected my chips. The second I walked into the room, Henna looked up. Surprise and pain flashed across her beautiful face before she schooled it away, hiding any and all emotion except indifference.

She watched me walk toward her, her eyes eating me up and giving me a sense of relief that she still wanted me. Eric talked about Henna being vulnerable, but I'd given

Henna more of me than anyone. Just when I was a few steps away from her, she turned to the other members of the table, said something, and then waited for the dealer to start the game.

I nodded my greeting to each of the players, two being Hollywood stars and the others members of well-to-do business families from around the world. There were eight of us in total, including Henna and me.

"Why are you here?" I heard Henna say in a low voice.

"You know why."

"I don't have anything left to give you. You took it all."

"There is one thing I want but we'll wait to get to that."

"Dammit, Zack. I can't." She shifted her seat as if to leave, and without thought, I set a hand on her leg.

It was as if electricity shot up my arm with a mere touch, bringing forth a craving for the woman who owned my soul. She froze and I knew she felt it too.

"Please, Henna. Stay. Play a few rounds and hear me out. If you don't like what I say, then you'll never have to interact with me again."

She sighed and nodded. "Three games minimum is the rule. Afterward, I'll listen."

The knot in my stomach eased. I wasn't home free, but at least she was giving me a chance.

We played for the next hour, Henna winning one round and me the other. This was it. I had to make this game last as long as possible and hope like crazy the last two players were Henna and me.

The cards were dealt.

Each player had unique ways of studying their cards. Some held them up, inspecting each one and then set them down, and others like Henna lifted the edge, giving their cards a noncommittal glance, and then waited.

Henna caught me watching her. She lifted her brow before picking up her glass of champagne and taking a sip. I wanted to fist her hair and wipe the smug look off her face with a kiss.

The round lasted for thirty minutes before players began to fold and the pot grew to well over twenty million. This was exactly how that night so many months ago had started. A high-stakes game and neither of us ready to concede. We were sharks who took risks and played to take it all.

Winning had been the best thing that ever happened to me. That one card game led to one of the most incredible nights of sex in my life and ignited a fire in my soul I never knew needed to be lit.

A slight blush tinged Henna's cheeks, and I was positive she was thinking the same thoughts.

The only way I was ever going to have her in my arms again was to lay it all out there. And if she accepted my proposal, I planned to clear this room and fuck her on this poker table.

"I fold. The two of you are like dogs on attack. It's fun to watch but painful to be in the mix," the last player, Zoya Petrov, a Russian heiress, said. "If you two don't fuck and relieve the tension, I'll be sorely disappointed in you. For a couple who aren't together anymore, your chemistry is off the charts."

Zoya rose to her feet and winked at Henna before gesturing to the dealer to follow her and walking out of the room.

"I believe I agree with her assessment," I said as the flush on Henna's skin deepened.

She ignored my statement and instead responded with, "I raise you one hundred thousand."

I didn't need to look at my cards to know Henna had the better hand. There was a look in her dark brown gaze that said she was ready to strike.

Time to lay it all out and see where the chips fell.

"I'll see you and raise you every asset under Lykaios International and ZL Holdings." I reached inside my tuxedo jacket, pulled out a set of papers, and then placed them on top of the chips.

CHAPTER TWENTY-TWO

Henna

"YOU CAN'T BE SERIOUS," I said, feeling all the pain and emotions of the last few weeks burn the back of my throat.

"I'm dead serious. You win this hand, all Lykaios International and ZL Holdings properties are one hundred percent yours."

My fingers trembled as I set them on the table over my cards. "What's the catch? I don't understand why you'd do this. You never do anything unless there is something in it for you."

"You're right. There's a catch." His sapphire gaze held mine as he reached in the pocket of his tuxedo pants. "This isn't how I planned to do this, but it makes sense it happens in the exact way it all started."

Zack set a dark blue box on the papers and popped open the unique container that was a signature of Harry Winston. Inside sat a platinum ring with a cushion-cut diamond that was at least seven carats surrounded by a halo of pink diamonds.

I swallowed as my eyes clouded with tears.

"I love you, Henna. Losing you was the worst mistake of my life. You are the only woman to make me want something beyond revenge. You are the only woman to make me want more from life than the next win. You are my future. You are my everything."

All the emotions of seeing him, of wanting him, erupted inside me. I tried to hold in the tears but felt the dampness on my cheeks. This man had gutted me and now he was really here. For me.

"What about Collin? He's a permanent part of my life."

"And a permanent part of mine."

That wasn't the answer I was expecting.

"What changed in the two weeks since I left Las Vegas?"

"I learned to forgive." He paused, setting his hand over mine. "I learned there are more important things in life."

Immediately, I felt the familiar tingle of his touch.

Before I could ask what brought on his change of heart,

he said, "I won't excuse all the shit Collin did to us, but I understand now. He was protecting your mom, you, and our sister."

I couldn't hide the surprise on my face.

"So, you knew?" he asked.

"Yes. It was an open secret my family has lived with for years. We only learned Anaya knew the truth recently."

Zack nodded.

"How did you find out? Did Collin tell you?"

"No. Hagen and Pierce did. They wanted me to understand why they'd reconciled with Collin"

"Then how did you find me? No one outside of Sylvia and Eric knew I was here."

"Your pal Eric took mercy on me. I was desperate, Henna. I had to find a way to talk to you."

I watched him, wanting so much to touch him, to feel his touch.

"You mean Sylvia plotted with him to get me to this game so you would stop calling at all hours of the day."

"Yes." A smile touched his lips. "I have to say my last conversation with Sylvia was interesting. Thankfully I was able to make my case and she agreed to help me. I think she and Eric enjoy playing matchmaker."

Of all people to have as my fairy godmothers, the last people I'd ever expect were an international mobster and a shipping tycoon who was just as dangerous.

"Zack..." I sighed. "I'm not sure..."

"Do you still love me?" Zack asked, cutting me off.

I stared at him. He'd shredded my heart. Made me believe that he'd used me. Hurt me deeper than anyone had ever done before.

"It doesn't matter how I feel." I tried to pull my hand free, but his fingers tightened around mine.

"It means everything. You're it for me. Tell me. Do you love me, Henna? I promise to spend the rest of my life showing you I'm worthy of it."

Could I tell him? Could I risk everything on him? Could I live without him?

My heartbeat drummed in my ears.

His head dropped as he closed his eyes for a brief moment and released my hand. He pushed back from the table.

"Where are you going? We haven't finished the game."

Surprise played over his face as did a longing I hadn't expected to see.

God, this man did love me.

Without shifting his piercing gaze from mine, he said, "Call."

I licked my lips and set my cards face up. "Royal flush."

"Tell me what this means, Henna."

"It means no matter what hand you have, we both win." I rose from my seat, came around the table until I was in front of him, and then leaned back on the edge.

"Are you sure?" There was such vulnerability in his words, solidifying that I was doing the right thing.

"It's more a matter of if *you're* sure. I won't make your life easy. I'll challenge you at every turn."

"I've never been afraid of your fire." Zack stood, gripping my hips and pulling me toward him. "Say it. I need to hear the words."

I lifted onto tiptoes, threaded my arms around his neck, and said, "I love you, Zacharias Lykaios."

"God I never thought I'd hear those words again." Zack fisted my hair and covered my mouth with his.

His kiss was all-consuming, filled with passion, need, and most of all, love.

He lifted me, setting my ass on the table. "We're getting married today."

I pulled back. "We're in Monte Carlo. It wouldn't be legal. Besides, you haven't even asked me."

"I'm not asking. You'd say no just to fuck with me."

I couldn't help but laugh. "God, I love you."

"Never stop telling me." He kissed my forehead, his lips lingering for a few extra moments. "You're my everything."

My breath hitched.

"Okay, you convinced me. We'll get married." I couldn't hide the joy in my voice. "If you call in the flight plan, we can be in the air within the next few hours."

"Where are we going?"

"Vegas. I believe there is an Elvis waiting at the chapel for us."

The End

Coming Soon - Master of Secret
(Gods of Vegas – Book 4)

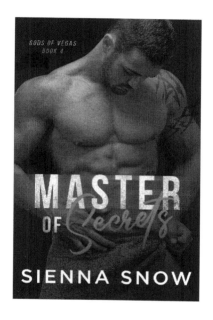

Preorder now -> www.books2read.com/masterofsecrets

Secrets are meant to be kept. Some forever. No matter the cost.

I live and thrive on deception and deceit. Manipulation is my game, and no one ever gets close enough to discover the truth.

Adrian Kipos is the man I cannot have. He knows

things that he shouldn't, and he has no qualms using information to his advantage.

One mistake and I'm on his radar, dealing with a man I should never cross. To keep him silent I must be his. Completely.

Nothing in my world is ever as it seems. Now I'm trapped between my own desire and my doom.

MASTER OF SIN

Read the first book in the Gods of Vegas Series:

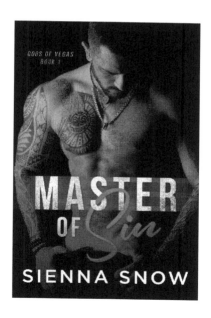

www.books2read.com/masterofsin

It was always him...

The one I shouldn't want, shouldn't crave, the one who could destroy my carefully built life.

Hagen Lykaios was the essence of sin, indulgence, and danger - everything I knew to avoid.

All it took was one unexpected touch, and he consumed me, left me begging, needy, and hungry for more.

He said if I entered his world he would corrupt me, own me, and change all that I had ever known...and you know what? **_I went anyway._**

ABOUT SIENNA SNOW

Inspired by her years working in corporate America, Sienna loves to serve up stories woven around confident and successful women who know what they want and how to get it, both in – and out – of the bedroom.

Her heroines are fresh, well-educated, and often find love and romance through atypical circumstances. Sienna treats her readers to enticing slices of hot romance infused with empowerment and indulgent satisfaction.

Sienna loves the life of travel and adventure. She plans to visit even the farthest corners of the world and delight in experiencing the variety of cultures along the way. When she isn't writing or traveling, Sienna is working on her "happily ever after" with her husband and children.

Sign up for her newsletter to be notified of releases, book sales, events and so much more.
http://www.siennasnow.com/newsletter
authorsiennasnow@gmail.com

BOOKS BY SIENNA SNOW

61534577R00148